Perdition: Ashfall Apocalypse 3

An Apocalyptic Thriller

M.L. Banner

Toes in the Water Publishing, LLC

ISBN: (Paperback): 978-1-947510-13-5

ISBN: (eBook): 978-1-947510-12-8

Version 1.02

PERDITION: ASHFALL APOCALYPSE 3 is an original work of fiction.

The characters and dialogs are the products of this author's vivid imagination.

Much of the science and the historical incidents described in this novel are based on reality, as are its warnings.

Prologue

Leticia - World Event Day 206 (63 Days since we left)

A lot has happened since we left what we thought was the safety of our home, so much so that I'm going to encapsulate—one of my favorite words by the way—two months of time in about fifteen minutes.

We had been tailed.

It was the Fish Man. He somehow followed us, snuck aboard our pickup truck and broadcast our location to the Polar Bear.

We only found him because we were in the Landcruiser, driving behind the pickup, and saw that the tarp, which was holding in the supplies, had come loose and was flapping wildly in back. When we pulled over and checked, we found Fish Man underneath, half-frozen in the truck bed.

After he admitted to everything, Compton, Joey, Ronald and Nan argued about whether to kill him or not. Chloe, Dog and I stayed out of it, which suited me just fine. I didn't like the man, but I couldn't vote for shooting him.

Compton was the most adamant about killing him. Compton said they'd be looking over their shoulders from now on, that letting this guy live was a bad idea which would come back to "bite you on the ass once again."

Ronald said he didn't want to be responsible for killing any more people.

Nan argued for leaving him on the side of the road somewhere, which I thought was the same thing as killing him. In the end, Nan won. Sort of.

Ronald, after the decision to leave him was made, forced the poor guy to strip. Said it was justice for what Polar Bear's son did to me. We drove him into some town off the beaten path, north of New Braunfels, and left him there. We then took a different road, so that we would bypass San Antonio. Ronald said this "would make us less likely to be found by Polar Bear's men." But everywhere we went during this new Ice Age was fraught with perils.

It was painfully obvious that the road we had chosen had not been used in months. After a few miles of obstructions and snow drifts nearly as high as our vehicles' windows, we had to turn back.

Ronald had us going to someplace in San Antonio, even though he said earlier it was dangerous, so that we could set up snowplows on each vehicle. He had a friend in town who had the supplies to do what we needed. Then the pickup died.

We had seen a light in a luxury development. So we left the pickup and many of our supplies, and packed all of us in the Landcruiser. That's when we ran across Steven Bigelow.

Bigelow was a rich guy who had run out of food and was trying to drive his RV to his doomsday bunker in Colorado. But the snow drifts stopped him too. We found him in the driver's seat sobbing and spinning his wheels, while attempting to dislodge his vehicle from some blockage in the snow. We freed him so he wanted to help us.

Turns out Bigelow had a full-service garage in his mega-mansion. He didn't work on cars, but he had lots of them, along with the parts, barrels of racing fuel and the lifts inside an aircraft-carrier-sized garage. We made a deal with Bigelow: If he gave us everything we wanted, we would protect him and take him to his bunker.

The pickup was unrepairable. And while we searched for his missing parts and more supplies, Ronald was able to fashion shovels onto Bigelow's RV and the Landcruiser, so we could get through blockages in the road and snow. We expected a lot of it in the higher elevations. Weeks later, we were back on the road with one more addition to our group.

Although Bigelow complained, which we found out later that he did a lot, we decided that we would first go to Joey's family's ranch in Arizona. It was a little out of the way, but we didn't expect as much snow because it was drier. Then we'd head north, dropping Bigelow off at his Colorado bunker, before we headed to our final destination in Wyoming.

Neither Polar Bear nor his men ever found us. Or so we thought. We did run into several more evil men, but Ronald and the rest of my new family dealt with them.

Until today, the trip to Arizona was smooth sailing, with little snow. Then a blizzard hit, slowing us down to a crawl...

I fell asleep until the gunshots woke me.

ENTRANCE INTERVIEW - PART 3

SUBJECTS: R. Ash, N. Thompson & L. Brown

The following is a compilation of audio recordings and interviews used to determine our case for being accepted. I have ordered these linearly to help you make your determination.

Thank you.

- Leticia

CHAPTER 1

Ron

When we realized we had driven into an ambush, it was too late.

Another new blizzard obscured our visibility to twenty feet in front of us. For this reason, Joey and Chloe led in the RV, which had only moderately better vision from their high seats and bigger headlamps. We followed their two taillights, which were like a couple of red fireflies that constantly blinked out of existence when we dropped too far behind.

Nan was driving, because she was pretty good at it and insisted so that I could rest. And I did until Nan called out, "Okay Joey, why are you stopping." She hit the brakes too, jarring me awake from one of my perpetual nightmares about Liz.

"What's up?" I asked, while aggressively rubbing the fatigue from my eyes. My right arm groaned from this action; I think I must have too.

From the seat behind me, Compton barked, "Pull out of his tracks so we can see."

Nan obliged, yanking the steering wheel right, pulling us up and onto the drift of snow created by the RV's snow shovel.

That's when we first caught a glimpse of them. They were like two ghostly shapes that fluttered in the thick glare of the RV's headlamps.

"They have rifles," announced Nan.

"It's a roadblock," said Compton at almost the same time.

A pair of headlights materialized behind us; their weak light flickered in our rear-view mirror. The truck they were attached to came to a stop not far behind us. That's when we knew we were trapped.

In front of us were two armed men and a blockade of cars meant to keep us from going forward. The sides of the road were impassible, as they were bounded by large drifts and rock formations. And the truck behind us prevented us from back-tracking.

"They've boxed us in," Nan huffed.

"Wha-what's going on?" begged Bigelow in the seat beside Compton. Steven Bartholomew Bigelow was how we got the million-dollar Mercedes RV that Joey was driving. He also helped us find parts for the Landcruiser when we desperately needed them, all in exchange for helping him get to some wealthy bunker condo-complex in Colorado. "Oh my God... Those-men-have-guns!" Bigelow squealed. He ducked behind Nan's seat. Yeah, Bigelow was pretty much a waste of air. But a promise was a promise.

"Shit," I hissed under my breath, while watching the two figures point their weapons at the RV's windshield.

Nan reached for the walkie resting on the dash and I put my hand over hers. "No," I instructed, keeping my eyes on the two gunmen. "Remember, we're conserving our batteries until we need 'em."

"I would think this constitutes a need," she stated. "Okay then, what do we do?"

I wondered this too.

"Let's give them what they want," Bigelow yelped from the floor.

That wasn't an option. If we gave in to these men, they'd take all of our supplies, and probably our lives too.

"We need to take out the threat," Compton stated matter-of-factly.

"Or we just drive past them," I said, far less resolutely. Engaging them seemed too dangerous to me.

"Nothing personal, Ron. But this is my wheelhouse," Compton instructed. "Nan, move us up slowly, alongside the RV."

She looked at me for confirmation and then back to Compton.

"Do it!" he demanded. I heard the loud clatter of him pulling back the charging handle on his AR. I automatically looked down at mine.

Nan jumped us forward, just as Compton asked. We moved slowly alongside the RV, our tires having difficulty finding traction, our snow shovel, just under the windshield, pushing the top layer of snow aside.

"Ron, rifle ready!"

I had my hand on the sling of my AR pistol and responded by pulling it over my neck. Then I followed Compton's earlier instructions for my Circle of Awareness. It only took a couple of seconds to check my magazine, confirm a round in the chamber, hit the forward assist, close the dust cover, and check the mag once more. "Ready," I said without thinking. But I wasn't really ready.

"Ron, we're going to slide outside when I say, while Nan continues to move the Landcruiser forward. We'll drop behind the vehicle until she stops even with the RV. That's when we'll take out the threat: I'll get the one on the left; you get the one on the right. You got me?" He clicked open his door, and a swirl of cold air rushed in.

One of the two gunmen—the "one on the right"—saw our movement and began stepping in our direction, his rifle also pivoted from the RV to us.

At this, I reached under the dash and maneuvered the snow shovel up higher, so that it would provide some protection if he began to fire at us.

"Get ready," Compton said.

At that very moment, an image popped into my mind of the first time I shot at and completely missed a target's head. And I was only a few feet away then. What if I missed this time and they got their shots off at Nan or Compton? I couldn't risk it.

My idea is better.

"Okay..." Compton announced, his voice washed away by a whoosh of wind blowing through his open door.

I jammed my foot down on top of Nan's accelerator foot, punching it to the floor. We lurched forward, instantaneously slamming Compton's door shut with a loud thunk, and we barreled for the gunman now standing directly in our path.

"What the hell," yelped Nan. She hard-gripped the steering wheel, craning her head to look past the shovel that obscured most of her vision.

"Aim for the opening in the blockade. Joey will follow," I yelled. At least that was what I hoped he would do. And that none of us would get shot in the process.

Out of Nan's driver's side window I caught a view of the gunman who had been in front of us, backpedaling out of our way. His weapon was pointed directly at us but he didn't shoot. The other gunman, behind him, fired off a round, but then turned his attention to the RV.

We zoomed past all of them and headed right for a small opening in a line of cars and trucks, arranged so that it was impossible for a vehicle to pass in between. We were going to ram our way through.

I lowered the shovel back down so Nan could better aim us and the shovel would take the brunt of the impact.

There were multiple pop-pop-pop sounds out the back, but I didn't hear the corresponding ping-sounds of the bullets hitting us.

"Brace for it," I warned. I felt her foot resist against mine. But I wanted us to get up to a high enough speed.

My eyes remained glued to the hole in the blockade and the RV's lights in the rear-view mirror. I caught the slightest glimpse of the RV, which seemed to be stuck in place, when we crashed into the blockade's first and then second car. Each car did a partial spin away from us, and we zoomed through the expanded opening.

"Stop!" I yelled, withdrew my foot from hers and spun in my seat to look out the back.

A cloud of white, made red from our taillights, billowed in our wake. When we came to rest, we waited for the haze to clear, and hopefully see the RV come through at any moment. The opening in the barricade was plenty wide for the RV.

When the fog of our actions cleared, we didn't see the RV. Beyond the opening, we saw nothing... No lights. No movement. No sign of them.

Only then did I notice Compton was gone too.

CHAPTER 2

Leticia

The clatter woke me from a dream in which we were almost at our new home, where Ronald and I would hopefully live forever.

"They're going to shoot—"

"Duck!"

"Woof-woof-woof"

I popped up from the table, where I had fallen asleep recording. I gaped at what I saw. It didn't seem real: Two men were standing outside, in front of the RV, with guns pointed at Ronald's blue Landcruiser... which was driving past us; Chloe was screaming and diving into the leg area of her seat; Joey was struggling to get the RV into gear, presumably to vanquish the two people about to shoot at Ronald and the others; and Dog was urging Joey to run over the two men or let him out so he could run over the men himself.

The rest happened so quickly my sleepy brain could barely keep up with it. Until later.

Is Ronald leaving us again? was my first passing thought.

I watched him drive past us and through the place where the armed men had been standing. Yet only one of them fired at him. Ronald's Landcruiser had a giant shovel attached to its front that looked like the yellow wing of a fire-breathing dragon. That wing was deployed higher than normal, and it swatted away the bad men. Then the wing lowered, and they aimed for the tiny opening in the line of cars that were blocking their way. The shovel-wing whacked at each car, sending them sideways. Then Ronald's dragon sliced through the blockade and disappeared into the murk, as I would have expected a dragon to do.

Our RV lunged forward toward the armed men, who then spun around and began firing their guns at us.

In my dreams, our RV was bulletproof.

This was a nightmare.

"Get down!" Joey hollered.

Our windshield exploded inward. My face was already covered, as I had ducked down, when something hit me and knocked me to the floor. I felt Dog's wet face on my neck. I didn't mind it this time.

The explosions were ear-splitting as the men continued to fire their weapons at us, though I was able to hear Joey use several bad words.

Then they stopped shooting.

Someone tugged at me, and Dog got off.

I stood and glanced at what used to be the giant windshield of our Mercedes RV. Now it was a gaping hole, with snow blowing inside.

I could no longer see the gunmen, nor the blue blur of Ronald's Landcruiser. And no one magically appeared in the blockade of cars to save us.

Joey must have realized this too, because he jerked me backwards, farther into the RV. Chloe was in front of us. Then Joey pulled me through the side doorway and for just a slight moment I was airborne, until I landed face-first into the snow.

Thankfully, to save on our gas consumption, we never turned up the heat too high in the RV. So I already had my winter coat on with my mittens stuffed inside. But my coat was open. Instantly I began to shiver.

Dog barked at someone, and I looked up and could see the men with the guns in front of the RV. One of them had a flashlight and was shining it inside the RV's empty front window.

The cold was creeping up my chest, through my open jacket, to my neck. My shuddering ratcheted up when Joey fired his gun right beside me. Chloe yelped, obviously surprised too. "Stay down," he said to us and squeezed off several more rounds at the two men, who were now too low to see.

Other shots rang out in the distance, but I couldn't tell where.

Joey told us to run toward the back of the RV. Dog understood. Chloe had an arm around me and me around her. My free handheld onto Dog's collar, as he tugged and pulled both of us to the back of the RV through the snow.

There was more gunfire, and we all dove into the snow. At this point, I was too cold to move. My body temperature must have been dropping rapidly, but I didn't do anything to zip up. It was like I was in shock from everything going on and my logical brain didn't want to work. Maybe it was too cold to.

Chloe was sobbing now. Dog wanted to be let go so he could attack somebody. But I was shivering so badly from the cold at that point, I don't think I could have let go.

The wind whipped at us, and the snow swirled all around, sending icicles of pain into our eyes. Even in the waning daylight, it was nearly impossible to see much of anything in these conditions. And now there seemed to be a complete absence of light.

Still, I squinted to see.

It was no use. The bad men either turned off their flashlights or they were too far away to see in this blizzard.

And even though we were somewhat protected by the back of the RV, I had the feeling that there were more bad people behind us. I didn't dare look. It hurt too much.

My greatest of fears flooded back at once and I began to cry. I was afraid that Ronald had left us; I was afraid that Joey had been shot, because I no longer saw or heard him. That meant Chloe, Dog and I were all alone. Chloe couldn't take care of me and Dog; she could barely care for herself.

My teeth chattered in synchronicity to my sobbing. I could feel my warm tears slide down my cheeks, then cool until I couldn't feel them by the time they made it to my chin.

Chloe's body was wracked by her own wailing. And then I remembered: It wasn't just Chloe anymore; she was pregnant and expecting a baby in a few months.

The cruel guilt of my own selfishness cut off my tears. I remember wrapping my arms around her, in an attempt to use whatever warmth I still possessed to heat not only Chloe, but her unborn baby too. One of my hands found the bump of her belly and I said to her, "Joey will be back for us. And so will Ronald. I promise." I remembered so many similar promises from my parents and other adults that I understood now were lies. But this was one lie I had to believe. There was no way I could do this myself.

My eyes remained closed, even tightening, and I let my thoughts go to Ronald. He wouldn't really leave us. He promised after we thought he was leaving us two months ago that he would die before he left us.

My teeth chattering stopped and I almost felt warm. My mind found some of my dream images of Ronald, when he was a knight in his suit of armor—I know it sounds silly, but they are my dreams. He had his sword raised in the air, riding his fire-breathing dragon, vanquishing all our enemies. I got completely lost in those thoughts, no longer caring what was going on around me.

My logical mind and the outside elements tried to pull back the curtain and reveal this dream to be false. My logical mind instructed me that we would freeze to death if we didn't move soon.

I chose the dream. What choice did I have?

Dog barked at me in such a booming voice, it sounded like he was using a bullhorn. I knew he was talking directly to me. He barked again and pawed at my shoulder so hard, I rolled off of Chloe onto my back. He pawed my chest and barked again.

Finally, I opened my eyes.

"Thanks Dog," I told him. "I'm awake now."

I rolled around to a kneeling position. Dog growled again. But this time it wasn't meant for me.

My eyes watered more at the stinging wind. Yet I tried to focus on whatever Dog was calling to my attention. It was so darned hard to make anything out... Until I did.

In the distance, someone was moving... Toward us.

CHAPTER 3

Nan

"Do you see any sign of them?" I asked, while eying the rear-view mirror.

Ron didn't answer. I couldn't really see his face, because it was nearly dark inside the cab of the Landcruiser, except for the dull light cast by the shovel controls under the dash. None of our other lights were on anywhere so as to not make us a target. But I could hear his hitching breaths... And Bigelow attempting to suppress his weeping.

"Compton's gone!" Ron blurted.

Bigelow meekly lifted his head above the seat back and turned to face the back window. "I-I don't know why you did-didn't just follow Compton's suggestion. He seemed to know what he was do—"

By the time Bigelow's second sentence left his lips, Ron must have been ready to launch a barrage of epithet-laden words at the man. Instead, Ron stuck out a finger and held it an inch or two from Bigelow's face. Even in the low-light conditions, he got the message.

I spun in my seat, not to address Bigelow, but to watch out the back window as well. I glared at the murkiness, attempting to will our people through the hole I had made through the blockade. But each moment of no movement consumed me with dread.

It had gone so bad so quickly. The snowplow was a great idea, although it didn't appear that the two armed men had even fired directly at us. And although I didn't say anything, I agreed with Bigelow: Ron should have followed Compton out of the vehicle and then taken out the two men, before they could have done much damage.

But Ron didn't and I couldn't help but wonder why. It wasn't fear because I knew Ron could be fearless at times. And it couldn't be just his stubbornness, his need to do things his own way... Perhaps he felt his way would reduce the chances of anyone getting shot. But in fact, his way and not communicating his plan to Joey so that they knew to follow, may have put everyone in jeopardy.

"We have to go back" slipped from my lips before I gave thought to my words. But I knew them to be true when I said it. We did have to go back.

There was a pounding sound, and I didn't have to look to know that Ron was beating his seat back with a fist in frustration.

"I'm going back," I stated with conviction and put the Landcruiser into gear, intending to spin us around and take us back through the hole.

"No!" Ron huffed. Bigelow may have tried to say the same thing, but he cut it off at the "N" and shrank back down behind my seat again.

"No," Ron repeated. "I'm going back. You two get out of the truck and wait for me to return with our people."

Bigelow opened his door, more than willing to comply with this order. I did not.

"And freeze to death while we wait for you to come back?" I said. "If you come back?"

Bigelow closed his door as silently as was possible.

"But I can't lose anyone else. I can't lose you too," he said, his voice cracking. "I just don't want to take any more chances."

I finally understood.

All his past behavior made sense to me then. He lost his wife Liz right in front of him. Then he lost his friends, our saviors, Bob and Sarah. And the whole time, Ron continued to tirelessly work and plan, all to protect us. But all that time, he tried to do everything himself. And all the time he kept everything to himself, never truly relying on the rest of us. Not this time.

"Ron, we are in this together. That may mean that we all die together. But I have a choice in this, same as you. Staying here or going back into the breach is my choice; not yours." I took a deep breath, attempting to fight my own emotions, which were raw at this point. "You've got to remember, we are stronger together, and have a better chance if we work together. And I fear, if you don't allow me and even Bigelow to help get our friends back, we won't have any chance."

Bigelow gulped loudly when his name was mentioned. But to his credit, he sat back up in his seat in a display of strength.

"Alright," Ron huffed. "But I'm driving."

Leticia

"Get up, Chloe," I whispered, one of my hands jostling her shoulder.

My eyes were glued on the lone figure, who approached stealthy from the side, getting ever closer to us. At first I thought it was Joey, but when the figure stood up taller than Joey should have been, I gulped back my breaths.

A truck door slammed behind us, and I swung around and twisted my gaze at the growing darkness. Someone was there, just as I had thought, but I couldn't see anything.

Then I heard a voice—a man whispering instructions to someone else behind us.

They were behind us, in front of us and beside us now. They were closing in and I didn't know what to do.

The beam from a flashlight moved in the direction of the man approaching us from the side, but I couldn't see him any longer. Dog continued his low growl.

He so wanted to be let go. But I didn't want him to leave us, or get hurt either. "Not yet, Boy," I instructed.

"Chloe!" I had both hands on her, shaking her. "Get up."

She wasn't sobbing any more. I had figured she was just trying to stay low and hidden.

Only then did it occur to me: Chloe was no longer moving.

CHAPTER 4

Ron

I hated it when Nan tossed irrefutable logic at me. So I told her I was driving and proceeded out the passenger door, intending to go around to the front.

"I've got shotgun," she announced and began sliding over to the passenger seat. "... or is it AR-gun," she said in a vain attempt to lighten the tension that was thicker than the snowstorm outside.

I jogged around the Landcruiser to the driver's side, dreading that our people wouldn't come through the blockade or what we'd discover when we drove back to find the RV.

After I hopped in, I saw Nan was following Compton's instructions by making sure her weapon was battle ready.

I put us back into gear and moved us around so that we were pointed in the right direction, and so we could better see if anyone, either friend or foe, came through the blockade.

"So, what's the plan?" she said. Her voice revealed only the slightest hint of nervousness. Even in the low light, I could see she looked heroic. Bigelow was another story.

His face wasn't visible when I turned to address him, but I could see his form shivering like a leaf, about to be shaken loose from a tree. At least he was sitting up in his seat this time, waiting for me to tell him what to do. I was glad he didn't have a weapon because he was liable to shoot all of us with it by accident. No, it was better if he stayed out of the way. "Why don't you stay low, near the middle of your seat and help anyone in, if they need it."

"Oh-okay," he said, fighting back another round of his endless stream of tears.

I regretted taking Bigelow in from day one. But at the time we were desperate. We had tried to outrun a gang of thugs, damaging the pickup in the process. He offered to help us when we needed it, along with the parts and a garage with power to make repairs. He was wealthy and had a full working garage, a working generator for power, along with a large, though now dwindling supply of gasoline, and finally everything I needed to fix the Landcruiser. In the end, the pickup truck was a total loss. But there were too many of us, along with our supplies to make it to Arizona in the Landcruiser.

So he offered us his luxury RV, on the condition that we take him along and deliver him to his bunker condo in Colorado. What he lacked in heroism, he certainly made up in generosity, even offering us a place to stay in his bunker, which he claimed had all the luxuries and over a decade's worth of food for more people than were scheduled to be there. Just like that, we were given a solution to ride out this new Ice Age.

At first, I was hesitant. But Leticia and the others convinced me otherwise. The RV, which was given to us, was perfect for us. It would take us anywhere we wanted to go, especially when I added the snowplow...

That was before I lost the damned thing. And maybe our people too. Because I was being too conservative. I decided then, if I had any choice, I was going to change this.

"Well?" Nan insisted.

I picked up the radio. "I should have done this sooner," I said to her, almost as an apology. "Hey, Joey or Chloe. Are you all right? Please report."

Silence.

"Shit!" I huffed. "All right. We'll go through slow and assess what happened to the RV and our people. If you see any threats out your side, do not hesitate."

"10-4," she said. "I got this. Let's roll."

Even though I was nervous as hell, I couldn't help but feel confidence in Nan there by my side. Like me, she would do anything in her power to protect our people, including giving her life.

"Okay, let's do this." I said and we each sat upright, getting ourselves ready to shoot any SOB who wasn't one of our people.

I put us back into gear, and we rolled toward the opening in the blockade of cars.

CHAPTER 5

Nan

Ron rolled down his window, using his hand crank, instantly sending in a blast of icy air. He moved his AR pistol from his chest to his right side, while gripping the steering wheel with his left. He lifted it up and rested the barrel on the window's edge and clicked off his safety.

I tried to do the same thing on my side, but because we had opposite windows, it felt like I needed to shoot lefty. I was naturally ambidextrous and the first time I shot a rifle it was left-handed, even though I was chided for "shooting like a girl." It was at a multi-family gathering during July 4th and the men found a box canyon nearby. It looked more fun than what the women were doing, so I tagged along. When it was my turn and I balanced the butt of the rifle on my left shoulder and aimed out my left eye, the joking started immediately. I silenced them all when I hit the target every single time.

Compton and Ron taught me to shoot this weapon right-handed. It came more natural to me, as I had done many other things as an adult right-handed. And now, unlike Ron, I could use both hands on my AR pistol.

As we rolled forward, I flexed the fingers in both my pistol hand and my foregrip hand, all to keep the circulation going to my fingers. Finally, I readjusted the butt stock, making it as short as it would go, and prepared myself, leaving my finger outside the trigger guard. Inside, it was getting colder by the second, but I was ready.

We rolled through the blockade's opening and the RV quickly came into view.

It wasn't moving and as we approached, it became clearer, and I could see why: The entire front end was shot up, the windshield was gone, debris from the RV was scattered all around and in front of it, and... There was a body.

As we slowly closed in on the RV, retracing our path, I sat up higher in my seat and twisted my eyes at the lifeless figure in the snow.

"It's not one of ours," Ron said, confirming what I thought.

"Do you see any of our people?" I asked, knowing his answer before he gave it. "No!"

There was no movement at all outside, which was surprising. I kind of expected to see more of the thugs trying to get into the RV or walking around it. But then I saw something that chilled me more than the Arctic temperatures. The entrance to the RV was wide open.

"You see that?" My voice cracked.

"Yep," he said.

There were more bullet holes in the side of the RV and in the door, which had swung wide open, and was flapping lightly back and forth from the breeze.

A pair of headlights turned on from behind the RV, momentarily illuminating its side, and what looked like blood amongst the many footprints.

"Must have been the truck that tried to block us in," Ron announced.

I leaned out of the side window and braced the weapon solidly to my right shoulder, aiming with my right eye. I scanned what I could with my left eye.

Pop-pop-pop in front of me; the resulting pings against our shovel sounded instantaneously.

I didn't hesitate. I squeezed off several rounds, targeting both headlamps.

Ron stopped our vehicle, leaned out the window and shot twice. But the headlamps were already out, either shot out by me or the vehicle's owner turned them off when they realized we were shooting back.

"Movement out your side," I hissed.

Ron pointed his gun in that direction and scanned for the movement, finding it.

It was more than one person, and they were running toward us. There was more gunfire in front of us. If it was our people, I needed to help them.

"Give them cover fire. If they're not ours, I've got them." Ron finished my thoughts.

I leaned back out my window and squeezed off two rounds at a time, knowing Ron would tell me if I needed to direct my fire elsewhere. I wanted to look back and see, but I kept aiming my rounds, two at a time, at where I remembered seeing the headlights, until my magazine was empty.

The side door popped open, and I could see Bigelow was doing something useful. While I glanced at Bigelow, I ejected the magazine and inserted another, punching the forward assist and then once again, I shot off multiple rounds in the direction of the headlights.

The Landcruiser shook as two people jumped in. Then the back door was opened, and I could hear Dog jump in, followed by someone else. Finally, the side door behind me opened, and in popped Compton. "Go-go-go!" he yelled.

I slid back in and attempted to roll up the window, but my hands weren't working because of the cold.

Ron, put us in reverse and gassed it, sending us back toward the opening we had just come through.

When my window was up, I spun in my seat to not only see where we were going, but to verify everyone was back.

It almost seemed too good to be true. Compton was there, wedged in between Bigelow, then a thicker than normal Chloe and finally Joey. Four adults—one expecting a baby in a few months—shoved into a seat that was barely comfortable for three. I could also see movement in the very back and knew it was Leticia and Dog. They were mostly obscured by the few supplies we had in the Landcruiser, stacked to the ceiling. Most of our supplies were in the RV, which it appeared we were now abandoning.

We were back through the opening in the blockade and Ron spun us around so that we were pointed in a way that we could leave from here.

Our group had made it. The supplies and the RV be damned. When Compton had jumped out—more like he had been catapulted out by Ron—he must have gathered our people and had them hide out and wait for us, knowing we would return.

Multiple people were struggling to catch their breaths, which made sense because it was work trudging through that snow. Leticia was suppressing a sob in the back and Dog was whimpering for some reason. Hopefully he wasn't hurt.

"Are we all here?" Ron asked.

"No thanks to you," Compton snapped.

"Eww, is that blood?" Bigelow sniveled, while attempting to wiggle away from Chloe. This was impossible because there was nowhere for him to escape.

That's when reality struck.

"Keep pressure on it, Joey," Compton instructed.

I couldn't see the blood, but I knew it had to be Chloe, whose eyes weren't open. "What happened?" I asked frantically.

Joey looked up, and through watery eyes, he said, "Chloe's been shot."

CHAPTER 6

Bobby McBoyd

I stood over my dead ranch hand, knowing I had to have revenge.

His thirty-year old body was riddled with gun shots to his torso, arms, and face. The boy's mother and father died bringing him to the Halstons, who rejected him until I took him in...

They'll pay for this.

"Damn, he looks dead!" announced one of my idiot guards beside me, rattling me out of my thoughts, but making me more enraged.

"Get the f—" I noticed that my idiot guard had brought one of his children here with him. "Make yourself useful and cover 'im up. Then you and Sloan get his body back to the house, while I check out the RV."

"Right, Bobby," said the idiot, who nodded as if the order finally sank into this thick skull. He then turned away and trudged toward Sloan, who had just arrived driving one of the ranch trucks.

I turned my attention to the RV that stood in the middle of my road, blocking anyone from getting to my place.

It was a beaut. A top-of-the-line Mercedes, which only wealthy people drove... Or used to. And this one was outfitted with a professionally installed snowplow. Key word, "was"... until my men shot the shit out of it. And why? I was going to ream Johnny a new one for doing this and getting his buddy killed... Couldn't you have shot the people inside and left the RV intact?

"What yah suppose that thing would have cost before the new Ice Age?" asked Scud, who had just stepped out of the RV.

"At least a mil," I said. I had no idea because it was way too rich for my blood. "What yah find inside?"

"Come in and look," Scud beckoned as he stepped back into the RV.

Scud was my number one guy, getting his name because, like a scud missile, I could send him anywhere to deliver my desired payload. He was first on the scene when the call came in.

"Look at all this," said Scud. He was pointing to the back of the RV.

I couldn't help but shake my head at the waste. My stupid men had shot up the inside of the RV; glass shards and other debris were everywhere. In spite of the damage, it was obvious that this was luxury RV-ing at its finest: leather and cherry wood throughout, top-of-the line tech and electronics, stainless steel appliances, supple carpet. But my idiot guard and his buddy destroyed it.

"Dammit!" I huffed, and then when I looked at where Scud had been pointing, I thought my eyes were playing tricks on my old body. And I guess Scud could see my disbelief because he said, "I know."

Through the last doorway, where I assumed a bedroom should have been, there were cases of food stacked up to the ceiling. And...

"Yes, that's a case of ARs and at least three thousand rounds of ammo. There are other supplies in there too."

It seemed too good to be true when we needed it the most. There was enough food here to feed all of us for at least a month, maybe more. And the guns and ammo meant we could put on a greater offense than I had planned.

"Who are these people?" I asked. Turning away from the supplies, I focused my attention on Scud, who I could tell had a lot more to tell me. He had a great sense about things, and I knew by his look that he had an opinion on this already.

Scud smiled. "I have only scratched the surface so far, but we know a few things about them, including where they were going." He walked back into the middle of the RV and snatched a book from the dining table.

He handed it to me. "This is the logbook of one their group. They have one of those ham radios, which they've left here too." I looked up from the first few pages of the logbook to see him pointing to a mobile radio transmitter nested in one of the shelving units above the table. "One of them has been speaking with someplace called Blackstone in Wyoming. I'm pretty sure they were headed there."

"But their license plates are from Texas." I said this while paging through the logbook. "Arizona is a little out of the way to go from Texas to Wyoming." I said this, but I was interested in the writing in the logbook. It was peculiar, because the writing was careful, like that of a young woman. I knew this from my Patsy's diary, which Wilma and I read often when she was downstairs to find out what boy's drawers she was trying to get into. This writer's letters were like Patsy's, back when she was a high schooler.

"I wondered that too," Scud replied. "Maybe they knew the Halstons and they were stopping by there first?"

I closed the book when I heard this. "Why the Halstons? They could be headed down this road for other reasons."

"This is why." Scud pointed at a map that was spread out on the wood inlaid dining table. It was an Arizona map with lines running from our area to Colorado and then off the map to an X, with "Blackstone/Wyoming" written at the top. In our area of the state were two little scrawls, in a man's handwriting, which read, "Halston/Joey's family."

I felt like I had been cold-cocked by my past. Could this really be Joey Rancone? Was he coming home, after what he did to my daughter?

I looked up and saw Scud waiting for me to digest what I had just learned. I suspect he knew exactly what I was thinking, as he always did.

"Does this mean we're going to hold off our attack of the Halstons?"

"Not at all. We now have more reasons than ever to attack."

CHAPTER 7

Leticia

They're missing! I thought and shivered at this and my hypothermia.

My logbook was gone and so was our map. And I knew they wouldn't be in my satchel because I had pulled both out and was looking over them when I had fallen asleep.

"I lost them, Dog!" More tears were coming, as I felt the weight of my mistake pile up on what we already lost: the RV and most of our supplies, our radio, my logbook, and our map to Wyoming.

Dog was whining beside me, and I thought he was mimicking my own whining at what I lost. But then I realized it had nothing to do with me. He was peeking through the supplies and baggage which blocked our seeing what all the commotion was up front.

The back of the Landcruiser had been packed so full of supplies and our bags. But when we moved some of them to the RV, it left only the space for one person to sit in one of the jump seats. Dog took up the rest of the room, now pawing at the suitcases that blocked me from seeing forward. He whined some more.

The scream yanked me into action. At first, I figured it was Bigelow, that rich guy, who always cried or screamed like a little girl. But then I realized it sounded more like

Nan. And since Nan never screamed, it scared me. I pulled the top suitcase out of the pile and it thunked behind us, as Dog and I pulled ourselves up to the ceiling to see over the next suitcase.

Nan kept turning around in her seat. She looked frantic... No, terrified.

"Help me, Dog, with the next one," I said pulling at the handle of the next bag. Dog pawed at this one too, and the bag came loose and fell on top of me, knocking me to the floor.

Of course, Dog slunk away at the right moment, avoiding any injury. I, on the other hand, had the wind knocked out of me.

I watched Dog jump on the seat and look over the next bag. He whimpered even more.

Something was very wrong, and I didn't really want to see, because I knew it had to be Chloe.

When she wasn't moving, I thought she had fainted. Women who couldn't handle things in my books always fainted. When Compton and Joey arrived, Joey scooped Chloe up and we followed Compton through the snow drifts and the darkness, until we could see Ronald return to get us.

The whole time, I didn't worry about Chloe, because Joey had her and he didn't say anything until just before we entered the Landcruiser. I had thought I heard him say she had something a lot. And figured he was saying that Chloe had been through a lot.

Could he have said, "She's been shot" instead?

I crawled past the heavy bag and stepped up to see over the next bag, right beside Dog. And I understood then.

It was Chloe screaming. She was in pain.

Joey had his hand on her swollen belly, and someone said, “Chloe's been shot.”

Ron

Nan screamed something. Leticia was sobbing. Compton told Joey to keep the pressure on both sides of the wound. I glanced again at Chloe, who looked so frail and near death and I thought, I've lost someone else.

"Will she survive?" I barked at Compton, keeping my eyes on the snowy road in front of me, watching for the sign Joey told me to watch for. I moved the rear-view mirror so I could see Chloe.

Compton said nothing, his hand on her neck, and then he pulled it away. His grim look said it all.

"Say something, dammit!" I snapped at him.

"You should have listened to me and shot those two pricks before they shot back, instead of trying your heroics, which will probably cost her her life. And we've left our supplies, which will kill all of us sooner than later."

"We have some of our supplies, including some ammo," I offered as my feeble reply, though I knew it was a stupid one.

"Great, when we get hungry, we'll each eat a bullet, which might be a better alternative to starving to death."

I replayed the scene in my mind as I watched Joey try to hold back Chloe's blood from spilling out of her.

"This is not helping her!" Joey glowered at Compton and then me.

"There's-there's more," Nan stammered. "Of-of them."

I redirected my eyes from the mirror, and slowed to a stop.

Although not as bad as earlier, the dark and blowing snow blurred out the headlamps, making it nearly impossible to see farther than a few feet. Standing a dozen yards in front of us were a man and a woman, dressed in dusters, pointing Winchester rifles at us.

CHAPTER 8

Nan

"Not again," I huffed, while eying the two people who were pointing their rifles at us. At the same time, my hands went to my weapon. I looked down to make sure that I had put in a new magazine and there was a round in the chamber. Check.

A quick glance at Ron had me concerned. He looked a little unsure. But then he mouthed a profanity and moved his AR pistol to his lap, for easy access. He turned his head and looked over at me, his eyes searching the darkness for confirmation of what he knew had to be done, this time.

I nodded.

"Are we ready this time, Ron?" Compton announced from the back, without any hint of sarcasm.

"Yes," Ron said.

"I am too," I said.

"Nan," Compton commanded. "Once you exit, you hang at the passenger side and protect from twelve to six. Do you understand?"

He was telling me to protect their tails by watching what was in front of the vehicle, or twelve o'clock, and covering the area around the passenger side, all the way back to the rear at six o'clock. Compton and Ron would cover the rest. "Yes!" I said enthusiastically. Although I was nervous, I was glad to be included.

"Joey, keep pressure on the wounds and we'll be back quickly."

"Roger, sir," Joey confirmed.

I didn't want to even look at him or at Chloe, as I wanted to be emotionally focused on what was about to happen and what I could control. I could only do my job or worry about them. Not both.

Dog growled from the back. "Dog wants a job too," Leticia said in a phlegm-filled voice.

"Leticia, you and Dog watch the very back of the truck, from inside. We'll call you if we need Dog," Compton responded. He was fully in charge of this operation.

"Okay folks, on my mark." Compton's door clicked open, just slightly. I did the same. Ron clutched the pistol's forward grip with his right hand and put his left hand on the door handle, so he could jump out on Compton's word.

It was time.

"Okay..."

"Wait!" Joey hollered from the back seat. "Take over," he commanded Bigelow, who squealed like a teenage girl who was just told to grab hold of a bug.

"Joey, hold on—" Ron insisted.

But it was too late. Joey's door popped open and closed, and he dashed outside.

His hands were thrust up into the air, but rather than approaching with caution, he ran toward both the man and woman, who trained their Winchesters at him.

"What the hell is he doing?" Compton asked.

Ron and I were stunned into silence. The only word from anyone was an "eww!" from Bigelow in back.

I didn't know the answer either, but then the armed woman lowered her rifle, and so did the man.

Joey knows these people.

When Joey stopped before the woman and lowered his arms, the woman bear hugged him while still holding the rifle.

None of us said anything. We just gawked as Joey pointed at us. The woman dashed toward us, followed by Joey, and the man disappeared.

I clutched my weapon, just in case.

The woman opened the door, where Joey had been sitting, and leaned inside. "Let me see the wound," she commanded Bigelow, without acknowledging any of us. She pulled up on the bloody scarf Bigelow and Joey had been using and then Chloe's shirt, only glancing for a moment. "Okay, keep pressure on it, like you've been doing."

"Joey," she yelled out the door, "give me a hand getting her in the truck."

A large four-door pickup truck appeared beside us, while Joey leaned into ours and pulled Chloe out of the Landcruiser.

Maybe because of the truck's cab-lights, it was the first time I really saw Chloe's face. She was unconscious and did not look good.

Joey cradled Chloe in his arms and hollered in our direction. "Follow us back to my family's ra—"

The door shut, cutting him off, and they disappeared in a snowy mist.

CHAPTER 9

Leticia

Chloe looked dead. And it didn't get any better in our vehicle.

As we followed the taillights of the truck that took Chloe and Joey away, Compton continued on Ronald, as Joey called it, "ripping him a new one," although I still didn't know what that meant.

"This would have gone differently if you had followed my lead," Compton belted from the back seat. "What the hell were you thinking?"

"I can't shoot worth a damn... I pictured them shooting our people before we got them," Ron meekly responded.

"Well, that already happened, didn't it?"

"This is not helping our situation, nor Chloe's," Nan said.

"But it needs to be said, and you know it," Compton continued. "But that's not the problem. The problem, Ronald, is that you don't like working as a team."

Nan unconsciously nodded but didn't look at Ronald.

"There was no time," Ron said. "I had to make a decision and I chose to push through."

"You can't do everything yourself if we're going to survive together. And you must communicate before you take actions which affect all of us."

"Look," Nan said, her head fixed forward.

I saw it too. The truck pulled up to a house that looked like a huge log cabin, and it honked its horn and the front door opened up.

"We need to continue this another time," Compton said and Ronald grumbled something back.

"They're taking Chloe inside," I said and like that, we were out of the Landcruiser.

Dog ran through the snow excitedly, leaping up in the air and landing, while taking in a mouthful of the stuff. I felt sick.

It must be nice to be a dog, where life is so simple, and you don't worry about anything but when your master will return. I'd love to get excited about something simple like the snow, but all I felt was nausea and worry.

I must have been in a trance, because I was startled when someone grabbed my shoulder and said, "Come on Teesh, let's go in and get warm." I looked up, almost expecting my father, and it was Ronald.

"My father called me Teesh."

"I know," Ronald said. "Remember, you said this in the short story you wrote about yourself. It's all right if I call you this, isn't it?"

I forgot I had him read it. I had already forgotten his question.

We were at the front door, and an old man introduced himself as Trunk, welcoming us to his home.

"Dog?" I said, looking around for him, feeling like I lost him.

But I saw him and he was fine.

"What a beautiful dog you have there," said Trunk in the doorway. Dog ambled toward his offered hand.

"Come on, young lady. Let's get you and your fine-looking dog inside where it's warm," the man said.

Both my shoulders were yanked at, and we were inside a huge great room with a baby grand piano on one side and on the other, a giant fireplace and lots of people standing and sitting around it, trying to get warm. Minus the piano, it was the way I would have pictured a hunting lodge, but there were way too many people there. I was feeling claustrophobic.

Trunk was saying something to someone about Chloe, saying that she was going to survive her gunshot wound.

"We appreciate your looking after Chloe for us, Mr. Halston," said Ronald somewhere in the distance. His voice was mostly lost in a stream of other voices.

"Trunk, please. And it's no problem, Chloe is practically family. In fact, any friends of my nephew Joey are family in my book." He said this to Nan too, who was sitting by the fireplace, warming her hands, and nodding at Trunk, who had moved over there.

"And I'm hoping you'll take me up on my offer and stay with us for good. We have plenty of food, it's safe, and we could always use a few more hands."

He wants us to stay here. With all these other people?

I felt my heart race more than it was before I stepped foot inside. My head swam.

I had messed up everything: I had lost the logbook and map, with directions to our new home, leaving us no other options but this little place bursting at the seams with people. Meanwhile Chloe was shot. Even if she survived as Trunk said, she wasn't going anywhere for a while. That meant we were here to stay for a long time. Maybe, as Trunk said, "for good."

I felt like I swallowed a brick, and it was lodged in my stomach.

I looked up from my stomach to the room and noticed that there were black borders around my world. It was like an expanding picture frame was consuming the edges of my vision. I knew what it was, but I couldn't do anything about it.

The black edges pushed inward, consuming more and more, until there was nothing but a pinpoint.

I don't remember anything else, except someone said, "She's fainted."

CHAPTER 10

Ron

The beam of light slapped me across my face. It was a lighthouse, warning me that our ship was about to crash into the fast-approaching sea wall.

I searched my ship but couldn't find anyone on board. Every few seconds, the lighthouse's beam of light came around, blinding me momentarily and then disappearing again.

Around the ship I ran, calling out their names, but no one answered. Then I heard cries for help from the stern. I knew it was them.

But I had to remain at the helm, so I could steer us away from the fast-approaching sea wall. There was no one else who could do this. The waves crashing violently against the sea wall were my reminder of the peril we all faced if I didn't turn us around and save us. Still, I couldn't ignore it any longer. I left the helm and ran aft, attempting to locate the verbal pleas.

The light blinded me once more, even though I had turned away from it, forcing me to stop and wait for it to pass. When it did, I could see that the cries were coming from the water, just off the stern. The cries were coming from Liz, Bob and Sarah, then Chloe; each of them were drowning. But I could do nothing to save them. All I could do was watch as one after another slipped below the water. Gone.

Compton was now yelling from some forward part of the ship. "Leave them. You have to save the others." But when I looked back, Joey and Leticia were now in the water, and so was Nan. They were drowning too.

Compton was now beside me. He said, "I guess you killed us all." Then he stepped off the ship and disappeared into the bottomless water.

The bright light hit me again and I felt someone shaking me. I tried to see who it was, but the light was directly in my eyes, making it impossible to see.

"Oh good, you're awake," Trunk said, removing his hand from my shoulder. "You told me to wake you when I had an update."

I blinked at the flashlight he had pointed at me.

He turned it off and pulled up a chair beside me, as I snapped to a sitting position in the makeshift bed that was set up on the floor of a room. I did a quick scan of the room: All the other makeshift beds were empty; a glint of light worked its way through the pulled blinds; the embers in the fireplace struggled to cast a soft red glow, having long since burned away whatever wood was thrown in there last night. There was no threat here. But what of—

I turned back to find Trunk glaring at me, serious as a heart attack. "What happened to Chlo—"

He held a hand up. "Ms. Chloe and her baby are doing just fine. The bullet missed anything important."

My heart was racing, still fiercely thumping in my chest. An image of the blood and how pale she looked flashed in my mind... And so did my dream. So I wasn't sure if I was dreaming or if this was real. I thought we had lost her last night. And my nightmare seemed to confirm it. "What?" was all I could say.

"Guess the bullet went clean through. It took out some muscle and other tissue, so she's going to experience a whole bunch of pain until that heals. We're monitoring for infection now. But Suzie tells me she'll be back on her feet in a few days."

"Thank you, God." I let out a sigh. "...and of course, your wife Suzie."

He nodded and continued. "Oh, and Ms. Leticia is fine too. Suzie said it was just an anxiety attack. Guess you folks have been through a lot lately."

A laugh sneaked out. "That's for sure. Just glad we found you when we did." I immediately thought of the two guys at the blockade, keeping my heart thumping longer.

"We are too. Just sorry you had to deal with McBoyd's thugs."

My heart skipped... He knew the men who attacked us. "Who?" I asked.

He kept his eyes focused on me, his face still stern, but a little smile sneaked in, as if the two men we ran into were some minor inconveniences, instead of two people who shot one of us, nearly killing Chloe and then destroying one of our vehicles, which we had to leave with more than half of our supplies. "I'll tell you about McBoyd," he said, "if you'll let me show you around and try to convince you folks to stay. I could use someone like you around here."

Joey must have already spoken to Trunk about me, which didn't necessarily put me at ease.

"And your lady friend too. Bigelow, not so much, but he says he's going."

Damn, I had forgotten about him.

"Yeah, he helped us out. And I promised to take him to some bunker he owns in Colorado."

"Heard that. He must have told us ten times this morning that he was anxious to get back on the road. I'm hoping I can convince you to come back here after you drop him off."

"I'm not sure it makes sense for you to take on more mouths to feed when you have several already and there's no way to make more food. This thing is going to last a long time." I didn't think it was right not being straight with someone who had been so helpful to us.

A full smile took root on Trunk's face. He obviously had an answer to this, but unless that included a gigantic storehouse full of a whole lot of food, I had no idea why he'd be smiling as much as he was.

"Come on, the weather's cleared up some. Let me show you the whole place, and you'll see why you should consider staying," Trunk beamed. "Suzie said she was going to show your missus the fields. They may already be out there."

This moment felt surreal. Even though my mind was yelling otherwise, Trunk's demeanor promoted a sense of calm. He struck me as sincere, but the "field" comment sounded wrong. As I was putting on my heavy coat and my shoes, I was filled with a sense of excitement in anticipation of seeing his "fields" outside. Yes, I knew it was a frozen world out there, and whatever fields he spoke of would be carpeted in white as far as the eye could see. But I was half-expecting it to be like summer outside, with green fields of wheat and corn going as far as the eye could see.

"I want to first show you our food storage. Then I'll show you our growing fields," he said, adding one more piece to the puzzle he was about to show me. He led me through a long hallway to a door at the end. Tacked onto that door was a piece of paper that read, 'So shall thy barns be filled with plenty." – Proverbs 3:10

CHAPTER 11

Nan

Bud is wagging his finger at me, as he always did to make me feel so inferior. Though I can't really see his face because he's wearing his old hoodie, and this time it seems several sizes too big, covering his whole head. He tells me, "You can't hide from it forever, Nanny-girl." His forefinger generates a draft that felt cold and makes me shiver.

"What?" I ask him. I heard him. I just don't want to go there.

"It's this!" he hollers in my face. And now I see him. His tongue is swollen, and his eyes are bulging. It's his dead face I see every time I close my eyes. Only this time his skin is undulating like the surface of ocean tides. Calm at first, but building up as it reaches the shore, until it's like a tsunami, crashing over the bones of his face, transforming into someone else's. I'm shocked when I see his face has become Leticia's.

"It's your fault everyone wants to hurt us. It's your fault Ronald wants to leave us," Leticia states, while she has taken over wagging her forefinger at me.

A clatter forced my eyes open, and I turned my head. I was awake now, staring at Suzie Halston, our host.

"Sorry," she said, leaning over to pick up a chair that had fallen.

"No worries," I said, making a show of stretching as if I had been up already, and it wasn't her that woke me.

"So glad you're up now," she said, walking over with the chair she had knocked down.

I glanced around the room, mostly to remind myself of where I was. We were not the only ones sleeping in this big room which, I gathered by the huge bed in the corner, used to be the Halstons' master bedroom. Now, there were six other beds set up around the room. Chloe was in one of them. She was talking to Joey, who was on one side holding her hand, and Leticia on the other side, holding out her recorder. Probably conducting another interview.

"She's doing just fine," Suzie reassured me. "And so is her baby. The bullet passed through with minimal damage. My only fear is that she won't stay in bed long enough to fully heal. She is a bit hyperactive."

My foggy brain just then pulled out the fact that Suzie Halston was an ER nurse. "And how is Leticia?" I ask. "She looks good."

"Ah, that one is just fine too. She's a resilient one," Suzie said with a smile. Only the faintest hint of a British accent came out then.

"Thanks for taking us in. We..." I felt a well of emotions come over me and found it hard to speak. "Just thanks." I turned away to hide my face before my tears could leak out.

"Honey," she said, putting her arms around me and squeezing, "you're safe now. You have nothing to worry about. And as far as we're concerned, you're practically family. We're hoping you'll stay as long as you like."

I don't know what came over me at that moment, but I started to sob.

After a long period of time, I stopped, and Suzie released me from her embrace. At that moment, I felt the same shame as I did when I woke up in that room after being abused by my husband and his men. And I couldn't help but think that thought that has been plaguing me every time we experience trouble.

"You are safe here with us, Nanette." Her voice was filled with compassion.

"Please call me Nan. I know you mean well, and I appreciate it. But I don't think I'll be safe, or maybe the rest of us will be safe, because of me."

Suzie tilted her head and her brows furrowed. "Nonsense! You were not the cause of McBoyd's attempt to take what wasn't his to take, just as you weren't responsible for any of the other mixed-up folks out there who hurt you before. And you are safer here than anywhere else out there."

She was sweet and meant well, but she didn't understand. So I tried to explain. "What's the term when God has subjected you to an eternal punishment because of your past sins? That's what we're experiencing, and all because of me."

"You're speaking of Perdition? Honey, maybe you should speak to my husband about that. He's the former pastor. That's more his area of expertise than mine. But I do know this..." She looked deep into my eyes. "No one, including you, Nan, or me, is worthy of salvation because of our sins. We should all be cast into the fires of Hell for our sins. But every person, including you, will be granted salvation if you ask Him."

She let that sit with me for a moment and then she stood up. "Come, Nan. Let me show you around the place and show you why you'll be safe here.

She turned away, and I swung out of my bed and stepped into my jeans, contemplating her words.

Part of me still couldn't shake the thought that I was in this state of Perdition. And that I had brought it on myself. And that everyone around me was subject to this state because of me. But the logical side of me accepted what she explained as well. I learned this in Sunday school after all. So it made sense.

I wanted to explore the discussion further, but I could see that Suzie was ready to do some show and tell.

And for the first time in a long time, I was starting to feel at ease.

Ron

"You do have an excellent supply of food and other provisions," I told him as he closed the door behind him, checking the lock to make sure it was engaged. "But what I don't understand is how you expect to add to this supply of food. And where are the animals you referred to earlier?"

Trunk flashed the same knowing smile he did earlier. It was as if he had the perfect answer to my question and couldn't wait to reveal it to me. Why did I have the feeling that once he did, I would feel compelled to buy into what he was selling? He reminded me of an evangelical preacher, about to reveal Jesus as the answer to all of the Earth's woes.

"Son, patience and all will be revealed." He walked past me. "Come on back through the house and then I'll take you out to the growing fields and show you why I have such faith in the bounty He has provided us and why there is more than enough for all of you as well."

Yep, just like a preacher.

We were halfway through the house when we heard Compton state, in a rather loud voice, "I'm leaving. These supplies are theirs."

CHAPTER 12

Nan

"What do you mean you're leaving?" Ron hollered across the living room, his face red with fury.

Compton had just deposited a shrink-wrapped food package onto the floor, beside a pile of similar looking supplies. They all looked like they had come from our truck. Compton stopped for a moment to glance up at Ron, and then at me.

I couldn't believe what I was hearing.

Compton looked like he wasn't going to say anything, but instead, he huffed out a sigh and then, "I'm not going to do this. Tell Leticia I left her a recording last night in her bag that explains why I'm leaving. Be well, folks." He turned and stepped out the front door, shutting it behind him.

Did he say what I think he said? It seemed impossible. The mystery man, who never spoke about himself when pressed, but who had saved our bacon in our long journey to Arizona. A thousand questions surfaced: Was he serious? How would he leave? And the big one... Why? But as quickly as my mind begged the questions, I knew the answers: Yes, he is; in our Landcruiser; it was because of Ron.

While I stood in shock, wrestling with those questions, Ron had marched across the room at a diagonal. He flew out the door, while zipping up his coat, and slammed it shut. I scurried after both.

I could hear Ron yell from behind the door, "You're not going to talk to us?" From what I knew about Compton, he wasn't going to talk to Ron. He was as stubborn as Ron: When he made up his mind, nothing was going to convince him otherwise. And from what I knew of Ron, he wouldn't stop pressing until something happened. Compton was a scab that Ron would pick at until it started to bleed. That was what I was afraid of when I opened the door.

"Are we gonna have a fight?" asked one of Trunk's workers, whose name I'd already forgotten.

"No, Carl. Just two guys working out their problems by discussing them," Trunk answered, now headed for the door too. Perhaps he wasn't so sure.

I was out the door first, followed by a line of people, including Suzie, Trunk, Carl—who was looking for a fight—and a few others I still didn't know.

Ron was stomping after Compton, who was headed to our Landcruiser. "And where do you think you're going in my Landcruiser?"

Compton stopped and turned to face Ron's oncoming fury. "I could have taken everything and left you people to die."

Ron kept coming.

"Ron, don't push me," Compton commanded. "I am taking this vehicle, along with four weeks' worth of supplies, one rifle and a hundred rounds of ammo. But

I am leaving you the rest of the supplies and in a safer place than the one in which I rescued you."

Ron stopped a few feet from him. "But why?"

The front door closed, with presumably everyone who lived or worked at the Halstons' outside, except Chloe, and maybe Leticia.

Ron and Compton were face to face. But Ron looked deflated, and Compton looked more frustrated than angry.

"What did I miss?" Joey asked from behind us.

"Shhh," someone responded.

"Ron, I wasn't going to do this... It's you. You're their leader, but you're too afraid to lead. You're not afraid of your own skin, but you are afraid of everyone else's. So much so that you make poor decisions. And then to top it off, you fail to communicate your decisions to your team members, so they can better assist you. This puts everyone, including me, in peril. You will not change, and I'm not sure you want to... That is, until you finally come to terms with the fact that you cannot save everyone. Last, you need to rely on your fellow team members to do what each of them are skilled to do. If you don't change, you'll lose more than just me."

He motioned like he was about to leave, but then added, "I am sorry, Ron. I just do not have the patience to teach you these things. So I cannot remain here with you as leader."

Compton hesitated again, perhaps this time waiting for Ron to respond, though I'm not sure how he could. Ron stood there as if he had received a series of gut punches from the heavyweight champion of gut punching. He just stared at Compton silently, as if he were waiting for another series of body blows.

Finally, Compton spun on his heels, probably intending to walk over to the driver's side door, before Ron spoke up. "But... How do you do this?" Ron asked, barely above a whisper. "How do you not worry about everyone, when everyday our lives are pushed so perilously close to ending?" Ron lifted his arms in the air. "How do you turn that off?"

"I don't know what to tell you, Ron. It's not my place to tell you how to do this. You'll have to figure that out on your own. Maybe you should ask your friends."

Ron took a step closer to Compton. "But how did you not worry about loved ones in combat? I cannot deal with losing another person I care about. I just can't."

"You just do. People die; that's what they do. You'll have to figure your own shit out, my friend. I never got emotionally attached to anyone: I've not had girlfriends, no wives, no kids, and other than my team members, I've had no friends... Not even pets!" He looked over to us. "Ron, in many ways you and I are not so different. Perhaps you should ask yourself why you cannot choose a name for your own dog."

Compton climbed into the Landcruiser, leaving Ron standing where he was, seemingly paralyzed from the dressing down he'd just received.

A distant noise blew in with the wind, causing some of us to redirect our attention down Halston's long driveway. It was another vehicle zooming toward us, followed by a swirl of snow trailing behind... It was honking its horn.

Compton had already taken up residence behind the Landcruiser's driver's seat, but he had left his door open. Ron had turned to face the oncoming vehicle.

The vehicle looked familiar. It was the four-door truck that picked up Chloe last night, the one that we followed to Halston's. The one-ton pickup had an even bigger camper shell attached to its bed. It slid to a stop just a few feet from us and a rush of snow and ice followed. Everyone turned away from the oncoming Arctic blast to shield themselves.

"Trunk," the driver yelled, "it's TJ. He's been killed." The driver disappeared behind the truck, while the front passenger jumped out and jogged to the back.

"Oh no," Suzie screeched. She and Trunk dashed to the back of the truck, with the rest of the crowd forgetting about Ron and Compton's one-way verbal battle.

I had no idea who TJ was, but he or she seemed to be someone important to Suzie and Trunk.

"Thought he worked for the enemy," said someone I couldn't see.

We congregated around the back of the truck as the driver and passenger pulled a dead man out of the camper.

They lowered him onto the icy driveway, and it was immediately obvious the man had been shot several times.

Suzie started to cry.

The driver handed Trunk a folded piece of paper. "This was shoved in his shirt pocket."

I heard Joey ask, "Who was this guy?"

And then another voice responded, "It's their nephew. But he worked for McBoyd, our enemy."

I didn't know who McBoyd was, but I heard his name mentioned a few times by Trunk last night. As in, "Was this McBoyd's handiwork? Or are you sure it was McBoyd?

Trunk read the note and he huffed out a sigh. He then folded it and put it into his own coat pocket.

"What does the note say, Trunk?" Suzie asked. "You might as well tell everyone, as I'm guessing it affects all of us."

Trunk glared at her and then yanked the paper back out and read from it. "McBoyd says," he projected his voice out so everyone could hear, "he's attacking us tomorrow if we don't give up our springs."

CHAPTER 13

Ron

"I recognize this person," Compton stated in his usual nonchalant manner to those of us surrounding TJ's body.

We'd all been chattering in hushed tones. Then everyone's words slowly dropped off.

"Mr. Compton," Trunk twisted his torso toward us, so he could see Compton. "How could you possibly know, TJ? You just arrived last night."

The funny thing was I recognized the man too, through his coat. Although marred by several holes and some blood—less than I would have expected based on the number of holes—the yellow and white coat was worn by one of the two men we encountered last night. This one, Nan would have run over or skewered with the Landcruiser's snow shovel if he hadn't jumped out of the way at the last second.

"I recognize him, because I was the one who shot him," Compton replied.

"Why?" Suzie wailed, as she caressed TJ's cheek with a hand.

"This man," Compton pointed at TJ, "was firing at my people and then at me." He said this to Suzie, then his voice trailed away. "The other one ran away before I could get him."

Nan had pulled up alongside me, pressing against me, craning her neck to see better.

"Yes, I'm pretty sure this is the man who shot at us," Nan proclaimed. "I almost ran him over."

"Sweet boy," Suzie mumbled under her breath, now hunkered over him, seemingly oblivious to our side conversations. She kissed his frozen cheek.

"I'm sorry," Nan glared at Suzie. "Was TJ one of yours?"

"Actually, yes," Trunk said, stepping closer to TJ, in between us and his wife, probably to spare Suzie from having to answer. "He's our nephew, my wife's sister's boy. But we haven't seen him for a few months." He looked up and pondered something. "He left for McBoyd's just after the ash started falling."

There was that name again.

The McBoyd name had been mentioned multiple times since we first arrived. Trunk had said the name and promised to explain who this was but had not yet had the chance. Or was he unwilling because he knew this was coming?

Compton seemed to be scrutinizing Trunk, then it looked like he had come to a decision. "Whomever this McBoyd is, do you have the means to defend against whatever attack this McBoyd intends to carry out tomorrow?"

Trunk looked over at Suzie, who gazed up at him through her flooded eyes, then back at Compton. "Afraid not. McBoyd has far more weapons than we do, and more men to attack us with."

Compton crossed his arms over his chest and scowled. "How could you possibly know how many weapons McBoyd's group possesses and how many men he has to fight with?" Compton asked.

"From TJ. He had been feeding us information, until recently." Trunk flashed a look at the lifeless figure on the ground.

I had that sinking feeling again and could not help but wonder what kind of hot, stinking mess we had found ourselves in the middle of this time. And in spite of all the back and forth, no one was asking the two most important questions. So I did. "Trunk, I think it's time you tell us who this McBoyd is, and what does he want so badly that he's willing to attack you, and I would assume kill you to get it?"

"I was going to ask this as well," Joey stated, now next to Nan.

Suzie stood up and wiped her eyes. Her demeanor had changed just then. She pulled on an edge of her coat and her face grew stern. "They have a right to know what they're getting into... If they choose to stay."

Trunk put an arm around her. "Well..." Trunk said, addressing our group, minus Chloe and Leticia, who were still inside. "This feud stretches back four generations to our great-grandparents, who originally settled this area.

"Each family owns two large but fairly equal sized tracks of land, bisected by a river. For the first three generations, the river was the center of the dispute as the Halstons and McBoyds fought over who owned what at that time was the most precious, the water rights.

"For the most part, our family had the better end of this battle, as our land was more verdant and lower-lying than the McBoyds', and we've had other wealth besides our land. The McBoyds have struggled since the beginning of time. So some of this feud is jealousy."

"Jealousy?" Compton laughed. "Sounds like there's quite a bit more to his threat than his just being jealous about your wealth."

"Tell them, Trunk. They need to know," Suzie stated.

"Wait, you said springs earlier," Nan interrupted. "The note demanded that you give up 'the springs.' I remember this because it sounded weird."

I wondered about this as well.

"It's hard to describe," Trunk said, scratching a cheek and looking back up to the sky for guidance.

"Perhaps you had better show them," Suzie said. "Only then will they see why our property is so valuable now, compared to any other time in history. And they'll also understand why McBoyd would do anything to possess it."

"Yep." Trunk smiled at Suzie and then stated in an elevated voice, "Come on, folks. Would you please follow me?" Then he turned to Compton. "Mr. Compton, you're welcome to come along too, if we're not keeping you."

If Compton caught the dig, he didn't show it. He trailed behind Trunk, along with the rest of us.

We walked around the side of the house and then along a path clear of snow, which stretched back, rising up to a flat field of white. In the distance were several interconnected steel buildings. The path appeared to take us directly to them.

Our group slowly made our way, as a series of gusts of cold air slapped at our exposed skin. I remember thinking maybe God was trying to slap some sense into us. Because the smartest course was for all of us to pile into the Landcruiser, with or without Compton, and leave this place before tomorrow morning.

I just had no idea what we were about to see, nor that it would change everything.

CHAPTER 14

Nan

I remember being so shocked at what I saw, I couldn't even speak.

I don't think any of us had any idea what Trunk was going to show us. So with a sense of both eagerness and anxiety, one by one, we followed Trunk into the closest of a group of enormous two-story buildings. Each was so close to the other they seemed to connect like giant Lego building blocks, set on wide fields of white. Not long ago, those fields would have flowed with golden corn, soybeans, and other cash crops. The buildings couldn't have seemed more out of place if they had been multi-colored, like Legos.

The first building Trunk led us through was filled, floor to ceiling, with machinery on both sides of a bisecting walkway. It was loud with a constant hissing and a steady mechanical hum. And it was warm inside. Surprisingly warm, in fact. But there was something else...

It smelled of sulfur.

The only reason I even knew what sulfur smelled like was because of the ash fall from months earlier. Ron explained that I was smelling sulfur from the volcanic emissions in our atmosphere, and the falling ash itself.

But there was no ash here. The machinery looked fairly clean and sounded as if it was operating smoothly. Not that I could really tell if it wasn't. I had no idea what this was.

Ron was behind me. So I looked back to catch his reaction, and maybe to ask him for some commentary. He was sporting the strangest expression, which told me that he understood exactly what this was. Seeing me stare, he flashed a knowing smile. My mouth opened, as I intended to ask him to explain, when Trunk announced farther forward, "Come on, you two. I want to close the door."

We hurried down the path, through the machine building, and stepped up and into a hall and then a doorway into the next building.

That's when I was so shocked, I couldn't speak.

I think all of us were, because no one said a word.

We stood on a slightly elevated platform and before us in a building the size of half a football field was a field of green plants and trees. Up above were grow lights, hundreds of them, just like Ron had set up in our little greenhouse. Only this was on a much larger scale.

Trunk, who was no longer wearing a coat, had his back to it all, and was fixated on each of our faces. He was enjoying our reaction to his growing operation.

I too had to take my coat off, because I was sweating.

"So what powers this?" Compton asked.

"Geothermal power," Ron replied immediately.

"Exactly, Ronald. I knew you would figure this out."

"You mean hot springs power all of this?" I asked. It seemed like a dumb question, but I wanted desperately to understand this. I knew we weren't staying very long, perhaps a very short time. But I still wanted to understand how this worked.

"It's so hot in here. How do you stand it and the smell?"

I should have known from the high-pitched voice, but I still glanced behind me to see Bigelow fanning himself rather than take his coat off.

"By the way, folks, you're welcome to take your coats off. That's what the hooks are for behind you."

I took the nearest to me and giggled when Bigelow made a production of taking his coat off.

"Inbreeding," Joey whispered to me and I giggled some more. It floored me to this day that Bigelow had somehow accumulated immeasurable wealth even though he lacked the intellect and the nerve to take any risk. It had to have been inherited.

"So..." Compton said to get us back onto the important subject at hand. "If I understand this, you have geothermal vents of hot air driving turbines in the other room, giving you power and heat... But for how long?"

"Well," said Trunk, "it's permanent." He began down the stairs, onto a path that separated the two fields of green plants and trees growing all around, like a botanical garden. I could see some were fruit trees. Some of the vines had berries on them. "Follow me."

"And I assume," Ron said with a raised voice, "McBoyd doesn't have this and that's why he wants it?"

Trunk continued walking and so we followed. He stopped about halfway through the field of green and waited for us to catch up. "Actually, the hot springs were on both of our lands long before our ancestors settled here. McBoyd had erected similar structures as these on his land to take advantage of his geothermal vents and hot springs. Although his were for a different reason.

"My plan was just to make my growing operation year-round. McBoyd decided he'd grow pot, as he thought it to be the next big cash crop. But, like everything he did, he was too late: The market for pot collapsed when it became legal for people to grow it on their own. Then his hot springs started to slow to a trickle and the hot air to his geothermal engine slowed. I even tried to help him and his engineers try and figure out the cause.

"But after the first earthquake, his vents and his hot springs stopped altogether. Naturally, he blamed us, as he did for every other problem in the past.

"When the ash fell, and the temperatures dropped... He started to get desperate."

Trunk began walking again. And we followed, anxious to see and hear more.

We marched into another building, filled with green growing plants. And then into another, and finally a vast field of corn stalks taller than Ron.

At the end of this field, Trunk marched up the next set of stairs, opened a door and disappeared into a hallway which was like each of the ones we had entered through to get to each building. I expected more of the same in the next.

We still couldn't see him, but as we continued our march, we could hear a flurry of muffled animal sounds and then a door closing, cutting off the sounds.

Our group pressed forward more rapidly to catch up and when we did, we were once again speechless. At least I was.

The next building was full of farm animals: cows, goats, chickens, and even several horses. All were sectioned off into their own areas, but under one big roof.

My first thought was to see if Leticia was seeing this. As an animal lover, she would have loved this. But I kind of remembered Ron saying that Dog was glued to Leticia, and I didn't see either of them outside or following us into the buildings.

I started to really think of Suzie Halston's offer for all of us to stay. Before Trunk showed us this, I didn't even give it a passing thought: We were on our way to Colorado to drop off The Whiner. Then to Blackstone in Wyoming, where based on Leticia's notes, they were completely self-sustainable. But this place...

I was trying to remember how many buildings I saw in a line. Was it four? Five? And each potentially filled with either animals or a year-round crop of something. And in spite of the cold outside, the operation could continue perpetually, as long as the machinery continued to run.

There might be enough for everybody... Except for McBoyd.

"Trunk?" Compton called out from a railing's edge. He looked down at Trunk, who was checking on the nearest goat paddock while we were busy gawking. Trunk looked up.

"You need to do everything in your power to protect this place. And I may be able to help."

CHAPTER 15

Leticia

Sleep helped to calm yesterday's anxiety attack. That didn't last.

Dog woke me up to tell me he had to go to the bathroom outside. This was not an easy endeavor, at least for me. I had to put on so many pieces of clothing to keep warm because it was so cold outside. Mrs. Halston, the nice lady who checked on me sometime last night, told me that Chloe and her baby were fine. I looked over to her bed and saw that she was sleeping.

Mrs. Halston also told me to be especially careful when I went outside because I had frostbite on my cheeks and neck.

I wrapped up so that only my eyes were exposed.

Dog was patient with me, even though I could tell he really had to go. When I have to go, I'm not very patient.

Finally, after much fussing, we were headed to the front door. "Hang on," I said to Dog, who was wagging his tail so hard, I thought it might come off. I stopped in front of the far corner of the Halstons' living room, which had bookcases stretching from the front door to the fireplace on the other wall, each filled floor to ceiling with books. Mrs. Halston said I could borrow any of them I wanted, and I saw several that caught my eye. Too bad we weren't staying.

Dog's groaning pulled me away, and to his delight, we were outside. He was happy and oblivious to the cold. In fact, he was so happy playing in the snow, I was thinking that his whole I-have-to-go-now act was perhaps subterfuge: he just wanted to be outside and play. But then he quickly did his thing and got back to playing. That's when I saw some of our group walking, following others, up a path that led to some big buildings.

Where is everyone going? I wondered.

Naturally, Dog and I followed.

When we got there, we had to walk through one building which was noisy and smelly, but no one was there. This was when my anxiety returned.

The rhythmic sounds of the building's machinery reminded me of how I was the one that messed up the machinery of our plan to find a permanent home. My mind filled with unanswerable questions: How could we get them back? Didn't we need to do this right away before we ran out of time?

Dog yipped for me to open the next door and we pressed forward, fueled by a growing desperation to find Ronald.

The next building, also devoid of people, was full of green plants and small trees. Above, a false sunlight blazed from hundreds of sunlamps. I should have been amazed by it all, but my anxiety had come back full steam. Without the map, logbook and radio, we could not find our permanent home in Wyoming.

One building, filled with green plants, after another. Then a field of corn. I heard voices up ahead and picked up my pace, hoping I was almost there

When we caught up with them, I was in a complete panic. It got much worse when I heard their discussion.

I didn't even notice Dog disappear into the group. He was happily ambling toward Ronald, who had his hands on his hips and looked upset. Our group was having some sort of argument, and I thought maybe if I listened, I wouldn't have to pay attention to what my mind was yelling at me. Boy, was I wrong.

Dog banged into one of Ronald's legs. He petted him and said to Mr. Halston, "So all you have to defend your ranch and your people is two Winchesters, fifty rounds of ammo, and a slingshot?"

"And," Compton cut in, "this is in spite of knowing a psycho, with many generations of blood on his family's hands, was always planning to take this place away from you?"

Mr. Halston was the target of Ronald and Compton's anger, but didn't respond to them. Mrs. Halston was behind him, with a hand on his shoulder. She was staring at me.

Compton continued. "Add to this the fact that you've known for a while now that McBoyd's group has lots of weapons and more men than you. And yet you've done nothing to prepare for this?"

I was feeling fuzzy-headed, like last night.

Nan piled on, "Don't forget, they have the extra guns and ammo from our RV that they took. So now they have even a greater advantage."

"Hold on," Mrs. Halston said, still staring at me. "Leticia, honey?" She let go of Mr. Halston and rushed toward me.

I must have been about to fall over because Joey was holding onto me. Then Mrs. Halston was there, telling me to breathe.

What a fool.

Like an idiot, I had stopped breathing out my mouth.

Nan was standing over me. "What's wrong, Leticia?" She seemed to know me pretty well, though at that point, I think everyone saw I was in distress.

The fog in my brain cleared. And I was standing on my own. Everyone had stopped speaking and now they were all staring at me, including Mr. Halston.

"I lost them!" flew out of my mouth before I could stop it. "The map, my notes and the radio—I left them in the RV last night when we escaped." I was starting to hyperventilate again.

"Those aren't important, Leticia," Joey said, trying to calm me. "It was more important that we got out of there safe."

"But-but without the map, my logbook and the radio, we can't find that place we were going to." I didn't say where because I didn't know if it was right to tell the Halstons about that secret.

They were quiet for a long time and didn't say anything. Each of my friends glanced from one to the other. It was just like adults do when they're all in on a big secret, but they don't want to mention anything that would give their secret away. But this secret was not the good kind. Even Dog stopped wagging his tail and glared up at the one who had stopped petting him. Ronald, whose shoulders were slumped forward, appeared to be confirming something from each of my friend's looks, before he turned his attention to Mr. Halston. "Well, I guess we're all staying to help you."

Oh no, I thought.

"You can't do that to me," Bigelow whined, his voice higher-pitched than normal. "You promised."

"Ahhh," Nan said, glancing tentatively at Bigelow and then at Trunk and the rest of the group. "That's all well and good. But we've already established that we don't have the manpower—even with us—nor enough weapons to properly defend this place. And it's not like we could barricade ourselves somewhere and wait it out. You would still lose all of this... So does anyone have any ideas?"

But for my heavy breathing, everyone was quiet.

Joey raised his hand, like he was in a classroom. "I do."

Everyone turned to stare at Joey.

"Well, speak up, boy," Mr. Halston said. "What's your idea?"

Joey looked at his feet and then back up to Mr. Halston. "I'm going to appeal to my would-be father-in-law."

CHAPTER 16

Ron

Joey went from pensive to downright embarrassed. His cheeks were redder than they would have been if he had just come in from the cold. We all drilled our eyes into him. I'm not sure any of us thought we had heard him correctly... Except Trunk.

Trunk nodded, confirming what his comment implied: Joey must have been engaged to McBoyd's daughter.

"Shit, boy," Trunk said. "Almost forgot about this other reason why McBoyd wants to seek his revenge."

"Trunk Halston," Suzie snapped. "You're not helping." She returned her gaze to Joey, only much softer. "Go on, son. You better bring everyone up to speed on what you did to poor ol' Patsy."

There was only one other time I had seen Joey like this. It was when Chloe let something slip, indicating that they had become intimate. Like then, he spent a long moment examining his feet before he addressed all of us.

"It's not something I'm proud of, but it's true. I was engaged to marry Patsy, Bobby and Wilma McBoyd's daughter..." His eyes were once again cast downward.

"And?" Nan gestured with her arms in the air. "What happened?"

Joey's brow furrowed. "And nothing. I wasn't in love with her. So I called it off."

Trunk snickered. "She was as fired up as a horse in a den of snakes."

Suzie shot Trunk a look that telegraphed, "Still not helping!"

"Yep, that breakup didn't help the situation none," Trunk said.

Suzie's shoulders squared to her husband. "So you would have been fine if the boy married a woman he didn't love, all because it would have calmed things between our two families?"

Trunk shrugged his shoulders.

She continued. "And some good came out of his breakup, because he joined the army."

"So Joey," I stepped in, as they were no longer addressing the immediate problem. "What makes you think that you can talk to her father and convince him not to attack?"

The red in Joey's cheeks faded. He addressed Trunk and Suzie. "If you'll remember, I was the one that had Bobby McBoyd bury the hatchet." Joey then looked at me. "He and I had a good rapport. Also, I showed him respect when I broke it off with Patsy by coming to him directly and telling him that I couldn't marry his daughter; that she should marry someone who was in love with her. Anyway, what do we have to lose by my going down there?"

"Maybe your life," I replied.

"No, I don't think he would hurt me," Joey stated. But I'm not sure he believed this completely.

"Bigger question," Trunk stated. "What makes you think he'll even see you? I know Bobby McBoyd's men. They're just as liable to shoot you before you make it to their front gate, much less to the door."

The entrance door clanged closed again, and I could see Compton had just returned. But from where I didn't know. I didn't even notice him leaving.

"I'll use Lover's Trail, the same route used by previous Halston and McBoyd family members. This was where Patsy and I first met and how we continued to meet up in the past, against your and her mother's wishes. I'm just going to hike the trail over and knock on the front door. If Mr. McBoyd won't listen to reason, perhaps his wife will... And if not her, then Patsy will."

One of Joey's shoulders slumped again. "Or is Patsy still pissed at me?"

Trunk smiled. "Probably. But don't think you'll see her anyway, much less her mother, Wilma. From TJ's last message, Bobby has them locked up in their rooms since yesterday, for their safety."

"Fine," said Joey. His shoulders squared up now. "If Mr. McBoyd doesn't relent, I'll go around to Patsy's private entrance."

"Won't he have any guards protecting them?" I asked, watching Compton come around behind Joey. He was carrying two weapons and a couple of backpacks.

"Good point," Trunk said. "There is at least one guard protecting the private entrances to their bedrooms and one guard inside the house. Other than the front gate, I'm not sure where the rest of them would be."

Joey looked kind of stunned. "I'll... Hell, I don't know. But I'll figure it out when I get—"

Compton grabbed Joey by the arm, "Come on." He handed Joey one of the AR pistols and a backpack. "You too, Ron. Get your gear. We are going right now to knock on Bobby McBoyd's door."

CHAPTER 17

Bobby McBoyd

"You take one of the Mini 14's."

Smittie—my freckle-faced nephew who was only a hair's breadth from eighteen—gave me his usual deer-in-the-headlights scowl. Then what I said registered. "Yes sir, Mr. McBoyd." The kid nodded and marched over to the gun rack to grab the last Mini 14. The rest had already been handed out to my other guards earlier.

The living room was my War Room, and it was bustling with activity. My men were coming and going. Danny—a cousin—was counting our ammo, which was probably unnecessary, as we had more than enough now with the addition of what we took from Halston's friends.

The battle plans were laid out on the big table, and I was standing over them just to give them one final review. I knew the plans were good and would be indefensible by whatever actions Halston attempted in his ridiculous efforts to hold onto what I was going to take. Really, all we could do now was wait. Meanwhile, I had my guards set up a perimeter around the property to protect against a preemptive attack. Not that Halston had the cojones to try something that bold. I expected them to hide.

I stabbed the drawing of the house. "I've finally got you over a barrel, Trunk Halston," I whispered to no one. I pictured what I would do to him when I had him as I continued to stab the house with my finger.

"What are you doing, Daddy?" Patsy asked from behind me. She should have been locked in her room as I had ordered.

I turned to give her the what-for, but I was momentarily transfixed. My daughter, the spitting image of my Wilma the day I had met her, was walking down the stairs, dressed in something like what Wilma wore on our wedding night. "Daughter, get some damned clothes on!" I hollered, shocked at her blatant misconduct, and angry that she disobeyed me once again.

She feigned surprise at my comment, while pulling the ends of her robe around her, loosely covering what no man, except a husband, had any business seeing.

"Answer the question, my prudish father," she said, stepping up to me and planting a kiss on my cheek.

Like her mother, she knew I couldn't resist her charms. It wasn't just her good looks that she got from her mother.

"You know how much I hate you parading around in your skimpy outfits with my men in the house." I almost forgot and snapped my head in the direction of three of them. They were staring at us... No, they were leering at Patsy. "Don't you have jobs to do?" I shouted.

They all reacted like I had punched them—which was what I wanted to do—and then broke for the front door, while mumbling in unison, "Sorry, Boss."

"Daddy, what are you doing?" Patsy squealed in her attempt to wrest back my attention. One more thing she picked up from her mother.

"Okay, fine! I plan to end the scourge known as the Halstons once and for all. I'm going to attack them at sunrise and get back what they took from me and my family."

At first, she fluttered her eyes. Then she turned serious. "But I heard Joey was back. You're not going to hurt him, are you?"

"Get back to your room, Patsy-Ann!" I commanded. "I won't have you pining for that boy again."

"But Daddy, I'm over Joey-macaroni. We were young and stupid. Neither of us wanted to get married. But we were being forced into it by you and Mummy because we were screwing like—"

"Would you stop it, Daughter!" I didn't want to hear about my daughter's sex life, much less that she had one, regardless of the fact that she was almost thirty. It was just her way to get to me, using her quick mind. There's another thing she got from Wilma.

I was done arguing with my daughter. Before she opened her mouth again, I hollered, "Redfield!"

"Just tell me you won't hurt Joey," she pleaded, her previous sarcasm gone.

I scowled at my brazen daughter, without answering.

Redfield showed up at the top of the stairwell. He glanced at me and then caught a glimpse of Patsy, who was where she shouldn't be. "Ms. McBoyd, what are you doing out of your room?" He trotted down the stairs with the size and elegance of an old bull.

It was obvious she had pulled another fast one on him, which was easy to do, as the man was as dumb as their dog, Millie.

Redfield stopped at the foot of the stairs and grabbed at the meat of Patsy's arm.

She yanked her arm away from his clutches and stepped back from him, crossing both arms across her chest in defiance of us both. "I'm not leaving until you tell me that you won't hurt Joey."

Redfield glowered at her and looked back at me for some sign of what he should do next. He obviously forgot my last order, that under no circumstances were either Patsy or Wilma to leave their rooms.

Again, I glared at Patsy, who was standing in her place so proudly. "If by sunrise, Halston doesn't give me what I want, I will kill him and everyone else staying at his house, including your precious Joey." I turned my angry stare to Redfield. "And do your damned job! Get my daughter into her bedroom if you have to drag her there."

Patsy gaped at me, letting her arms drop. But then her head snapped to Redfield, who had once again reached for her. "If you touch me, I will claw your eyes out, you dumb ape."

She turned and ran past Redfield, up the stairs.

Redfield followed behind her like a dog whose balls had been removed.

I grabbed my radio and keyed the mike. "I need another man posted with Redfield to make sure that neither my daughter or wife leave their rooms."

"Roger, Sir," said Scud on the other end.

I tossed the radio onto the map on the table. It came to rest by the outline of the Halstons' house.

CHAPTER 18

Ron

"Ronald," Compton made sure he had my attention. Then he looked at Joey. "And Joey. To be absolutely clear. You both will do exactly as I say, when I say it. And you will not question my orders in any way. Do you agree?"

"Yes, I agree," I said, trying to keep him from seeing any of the reluctance I felt.

"Yes, Sir," Joey stated.

"Do you have any questions about what each of you are doing?"

He really hadn't told us anything, other than what each of our basic roles would be. I had to trust he would fill in the details when it was time. That dependency on another, regardless of their obvious skill set, always made me nervous, especially ever since the apocalypse.

Both of us said, "No, Sir."

"Okay, take us there," Compton commanded.

Joey took the most forward seat on the long snowmobile, which resembled a giant wave runner, but with skis. I climbed on behind him, slinging my AR pistol onto my right shoulder. Compton followed, sitting behind me. Our packs were resting in an otherwise empty skiff, connected to the snowmobile's back hitch.

As Joey started the engine and got us moving, I thought about the risk we were taking, delivering ourselves right onto the property of this crazy man, Bobby McBoyd. We may have been outmatched in firepower and manpower against McBoyd, but surely it would have been better to build traps and draw them in somehow when they attacked. I suggested this, but Compton shot it down immediately.

He stated in no uncertain terms that he didn't want to get into a firefight with a superior enemy, that we were better off taking matters into our own hands. Further, he said that he wasn't going to argue with me: We were going to do it his way or I would have to sit out of his operation. Though he also said it would be better to have another set of eyeballs, my eyes. But only if I did what he said.

Naturally, I agreed. Assuming Compton didn't get us killed, I had hoped to use this opportunity to convince him to stay with us when we ultimately left this place.

Joey hit a hard turn and we had to lean into it and hang on for dear life to keep from flying off.

Moments later, we found ourselves in a canyon that was covered in snow and ice. We were stopped at the bottom, which was flat like it at one time contained a large pool of water. Surrounding us were rock walls a hundred feet high on each side.

"We are on McBoyd's property now," Joey said and then pointed ahead to a small depression in the snow that ran up the side of the wall in front of us and disappeared unseen, around a bend in the canyon. "That's the trail we're going to take. We'll need to take this slowly and as quiet as possible. But before the top, there's a place we can stop just on this side of the rise. I'm thinking they won't be able to hear or see us if we stop there."

"That's great intel, Joey. Thanks," Compton said.

"Was this a pool at one time?" I asked.

Joey looked over the long flat area that ran through the canyon and then disappeared where it narrowed, and turned to us, smiling. "Yes, and it was here that I first met Patsy McBoyd.

"It was a cold morning in winter—maybe thirty degrees—when I rode up on horseback, to this pool. It was formed by a natural hot spring. As I said, this was McBoyd's side, so we never used this pool, and we only used this trail if we were going to McBoyd's, which never happened while I lived here, because neither side spoke to the other. As I mentioned, I had never told Trunk, because he told me in no uncertain terms not to cross onto McBoyd's property, but I often rode through here because it was so beautiful. That's when I saw her.

"I remember watching as Patsy's head popped up out of the water, her eyes on me. Then she rose further, exposing her shoulders. Then she rose further, exposing... Well, I realized then that she was completely naked and she was smiling at me, like she knew something I didn't. She walked right up to me and well... One thing led to another... Um, you know the rest.

"Anyway, Trunk said that this hot spring, along with all the others on McBoyd's side, dried up after the first earthquake. And now, you can see it's frozen."

"So McBoyd thinks your uncle was somehow responsible for this?" I asked.

"Not so much responsible. His family just felt they got the short end of the stick. It sounds like the hot springs were the final straw."

"Thanks, Joey, for the history lesson," Compton stated. "But let's focus on the operation at hand. We can discuss history tomorrow, assuming we have a tomorrow. Let's get going."

Joey nodded and drove us the rest of the way up a steep trail head, barely visible in the snow, then to the area he had suggested. It was just off the trail, hidden by snow drifts and trees on one side and the open canyon on the other.

We retrieved our packs and hiked a short distance to a line of small trees. "There it is," Joey announced.

On the other side of the trees was an open field, leading up to a rambling ranch-style home with a two-story addition on the back side. A long drive shot out the front and disappeared to our right. And there were guards. A lot of them.

"Dare we ask now, what is the plan?" I whispered, trying with difficulty to keep track of the four or five men moving around the front of the property. It was hard to see them, as wisps of wind continued to blow the snow around, mostly obscuring our view. Each time the gusts waned and I caught a glimpse of one of them, it felt like he or she was looking in our direction.

"Yes, you can," Compton responded. But that was all he said. His point to me was obvious: You can ask, but because I'm in charge, I don't have to answer.

Joey snickered, but it sounded more nervous. He knew Compton was screwing with me.

"So, as you probably guessed," Joey said pointing to our left. "In that two-story addition, you'll find Patsy's room on the second floor and her mother and father's room below this. Both have separate entrances in back. I'm sure there is at least one guard outside there. And I would presume another inside, perhaps just outside one their doors, which lead to a grand staircase in the living room."

"You let me worry about the guards. You and Ronald are going to the front door. Try to get there silently. The guards won't expect you, so unless you make too much noise, you should be able to march right up to the front door."

He must have seen me fussing with my weapon.

"Leave your weapons and bags here."

My mouth opened and then snapped shut when Compton glared metal spikes at me. "You are going to the front door, preferably without being seen, and make your plea, unarmed. If you take too long or there is a problem, I will set off a diversion. We meet back at the snowmobile. But if you take too long to get here, I may leave before you. Just follow the same trail back on foot and I'll find you there."

"And what will you be doing, besides preparing a diversion?" I asked.

"I'll be doing what I do best," he said, swinging his AK pistol around to his chest.

"Sir, I have to ask, please do not kill anyone. I'm trying to make the peace and killing any of McBoyd's men won't help," Joey said.

"That's my plan," Compton answered. "All right, go now."

We did as he asked, keeping low, slowly trudging our way through the snow toward the front of the house.

After a few steps, I looked back and Compton was gone. I twisted from side to side to see if I could catch a glimpse of him, but he disappeared without a trace.

I fixed my sights on the front door, our target, and knew that this was a dumb idea.

CHAPTER 19

Leticia

It was pretty easy to sneak out while the adults were arguing about what they should do next. I was more concerned about what happened after we left this place, as well as shouldering guilt for my epic screw-up. No matter what happened, I had to get back the map, logbook and radio from the RV.

I grabbed my BOB and some extra gear for winter survival—Compton had instructed we do this if we were going more than five hundred feet away from home base—and quietly marched out Mr. and Mrs. Halston's front door. I also carried an empty satchel for what I could grab from the RV. Assuming I could reclaim the most important items stolen from us, maybe they would forgive me for my wrongs.

Once again, Dog was my trusty friend and protector. He was also necessary, because I'm not sure I would have had the guts to do this mission myself. Dog always had my back, as Joey often liked to remind me.

The weather was favorable today. It was the usual cold and cloudy, but at least it wasn't snowing, or windy. Still, as Nan liked to describe me, I was wrapped up like the Christmas Story kid. I never understood what she meant, but I laughed with her as if I did. Adults often liked to refer to scenes from their favorite childhood movies or TV shows. My parents made sure I had books.

The fading light added to my growing worry. I was sure I could find the RV, as it was right down the road. The difficulty was getting past the guards and navigating inside the RV when I got there. At the first blockade, I had to turn on my flashlight.

This was the Halstons' blockade and other than banging my head against a side mirror, we got through unnoticed. We were lucky that there was only one guard. Dog found him sound asleep in one of the parked vehicles, wrapped in layers of heavy blankets. It was the next blockade where we had problems.

I could see the RV through the blockade's opening, along with the guards. There were at least three. If we could get by the two at the blockade, we had to get by the one posted by the RV too.

"Any ideas, Dog?" I whispered, while kneeling to pet him.

He whimpered a little and licked my ear. Then he did something completely unexpected. He darted away from me.

At first, I thought he was going back, in hopes that I would come with him. But he ran around the car I was kneeling beside, and he darted through the opening toward the two guards posted there.

I stood up in amazement and watched as Dog woofed as he dashed in front of one guard and then another. The first was shocked and didn't react. The second yelped. Then Dog broke for the guard by the RV, who seemed asleep while standing up. Dog literally ran into the guy, knocking him down. And all three took off after Dog, who darted for the rear of the RV.

It was my chance and Dog gave it to me.

I ran for the RV's side entrance, while keeping an eye out for the guards. I could see and hear them scurrying after Dog. If any one of them turned around, they would surely see me. But they were so focused on getting through the deep snow and chasing after Dog, whereas I had a well-trodden path all the way to the RV's door. The same one we had exited only last night.

Once I was at the door, a quick glance around confirmed that I was the only one. The door opened easily—I think I expected it to be locked. But when I stepped inside, my stomach, already tied up in knots, sank.

Everything that was important was gone. The map and book. The radio. Our boxes of supplies, including the guns. All taken.

I was alerted to Dog barking wildly. I turned around just as he shot inside and then nudged at me. He wanted me to go.

I glanced around the RV once more, to see if there was anything worth grabbing. There wasn't. Dog growled and I could hear a voice, just outside the door. "Hide," I whispered to Dog.

The bathroom was what came to mind.

I grabbed Dog's collar and he reluctantly followed as more voices poured in through the door.

"I think he went that way."

"Hey, Johnny. Did you leave the door open?"

Dog followed me into the mini-shower, and I pulled the translucent door closed. We waited, as the voices approached.

The voices were muffled and unintelligible with the shower and bathroom doors closed. But I could feel the footsteps of a heavy man. It was the guard who was stationed at the door.

The footsteps grew louder. Then the bathroom door opened.

Before I could say or do anything, Dog exploded out of the shower and leaped onto the man. As he tried to escape into the bedroom, I rushed out. I tried to ignore the cries of fear coming from the bedroom, as I made for the exit outside.

I ran as fast as I could, hoping Dog would follow me.

My intent was to head back the way we had come, but there was a man there. One of the other guards.

Before I could avoid him, he grabbed me and slammed the RV's door. Dog banged on it from the other side, while I struggled to get free as well. But it was no use. We were both trapped.

CHAPTER 20

Ron

When Joey pounded on the hand-carved door, which looked strangely familiar, my mind was flooded with long forgotten images, and an overwhelming feeling of dread.

I was a kid again, trick-or-treating with a group of friends. After knocking on a door like this one, unbeknownst to me, one of my so-called friends was busy lighting firecrackers in a pile of raked-up leaves. The door opened as the firecrackers exploded and we dashed away. That October was dry. So it should have been no surprise that the leaves were a tinderbox and flamed up immediately.

My friends had already run past the pile, ignoring the flames which threatened to spread, and then disappeared into the recesses of Mr. and Mrs. Darby's yard. I could have done the same, but the pile of leaves abutted the Darby's old wooden tool shed. Leaves were one thing; vandalism was another.

So I leaped for the pile, thinking I could use my body like a blanket to put out the fire. Of course, it didn't work.

The shed burnt down, along with all of its contents, I sustained burns and ruined my clothes, I almost got arrested and I was forced to work on the Darbys' yard for two summers just to repay them. All because of the actions and plans of others.

Back then we were dressed as pirates, intending to plunder candy from neighbors, while one of our group was committing an act of vandalism. Now we were dressed like two survivalists, just stepping out of the wilderness, while one of our group was about to do something worse, which could get both of us killed.

I was about to tell Joey that this whole plan felt wrong, and we should abandon it, when the door opened.

I almost expected Mr. Darby holding a plastic Jack-o-lantern full of candy. Of course, in this apocalyptic world, it was a stranger pointing a rifle at us instead.

"Hello Mr. McBoyd," Joey said with a smile, his hands immediately thrust into the air. "This is my friend, Ronald Ash. We're here beca—"

"Joseph Robert Rancone? Is that you, my boy? All grown up and back from the Army?" An attractive older woman rushed toward us from an interior doorway, brushing by Bobby McBoyd and embracing Joey as if he were the prodigal son, having just returned home.

"Hello Mrs. McBoyd," Joey said with effort.

When she released him, Joey glanced at me and shrugged his shoulders. His cheeks were red once again, and he couldn't blame it on the cold this time.

"Wilma McBoyd, this is my friend, Ronald—"

A brown blur rushed by everyone and tumbled into Joey. It happened so fast, neither of us could react. When I saw it was a good-sized German Shepherd, I gulped back my already shallow breaths. But the dog's tail was wagging faster than a weed-whacker.

"Hello Millie," Joey said enthusiastically, while rubbing the dog's ears.

It was obvious Joey knew all the family members pretty well.

"Come on out of the cold, boys," Wilma said, stepping back to let us in.

Bobby McBoyd had lowered his rifle, apparently no longer seeing us as a threat. But the feeling wasn't mutual. It was one of my AR pistols that he was pointing at us.

Out of my mouth fell the words, "I see you helped yourself to the supplies from our RV."

Yeah, it wasn't the brightest thing I could have said. But I hated thieves and I let my anger mess with my better sense of judgment, and our mission.

Bobby McBoyd immediately took a step back and pointed my rifle at me. "So it was you who killed one of my men last night."

He whistled loud enough that everyone inside and probably outside of the house could hear him.

A rush of heavy footsteps immediately sounded relatively close, proceeded by the presence of a linebacker-sized man with dull eyes and a drooping mouth. Another two guards followed but held up behind the dumb-looking linebacker.

McBoyd didn't glance back to acknowledge the big man's presence, but spat, "Take these two to the cellar and lock them both inside. And if they attempt to escape, you are to shoot them. Is that clear?"

"Redfield!" Wilma waved to get the big man's attention. "You know my husband isn't serious about shooting these men, right?"

"Wait!" Bobby held a hand up, for either the big man or Wilma, I wasn't sure. "Redfield, better yet." He turned his head slightly so that his eyes were on Wilma. "Take Mrs. McBoyd to her daughter's room and lock her in there."

"Don't you dare touch me, Redfield," Wilma spat.

Redfield hesitated, glaring first at Wilma and then Bobby. I could see he had a small pistol in one hand, which I guess was meant for us. He holstered it and then said, "Please come with me, Mrs. McBoyd."

Wilma glowered at her husband. "You and I are going to have a conversation when this is all over." She turned and walked through the living room and up a flight of stairs, with Redfield shuffling after her.

The oldest of the remaining two guards asked Bobby, "What do you want us to do, Sir?" He also had one of my AR pistols, and the other had a similar-caliber semi-automatic rifle.

Bobby walked toward the living room and announced, "Close the door and make sure these two don't do anything they'll regret. When Redfield returns, I'll have him deal with them."

His back was to us, and I flashed Joey a what-the-hell-did-that-mean look. He shrugged and followed Bobby into the living room.

Joey stopped beside Bobby, before a giant table with papers spread out all over it, which upon getting closer looked like battle plans.

Joey glanced at the table and then Bobby. "You remember you once told me that family was most important and that I was practically your family?"

I could see that the table had an oversized plat map taking up most of its surface. It's a map of both McBoyd's and Halston's properties and the canyon separating them.

"That was before you dumped my daughter," Bobby huffed.

On Halston's side of the map there were arrows drawn at different points. These are the points of attack by McBoyd's men.

"But you also agreed that it was best that I not marry your daughter, because your daughter's happiness was more important than everything else."

By each arrow were stick figures representing each man attacking the grounds at each point. I mentally kept count of each of the stick figures.

"That was a long time ago... It was different then, when we were self-sufficient. But when the temperatures dropped and Halston stole our springs, everything changed. I no longer have a choice about what happens next. And nothing you say can change my mind..."

At least twenty men, with rifles and at least three t housand rounds of our ammo!

Bobby looked up at the stairwell. "At least for once, I'll give my daughter what she asked for." He looked back at both of us. "Don't worry. As long as you don't try anything stupid, I'll release you and your friend unharmed, after we have destroyed the Halstons tomorrow."

CHAPTER 21

Compton

When I slipped through her outside bedroom entrance without a sound, I caught a glimpse of her laying on top of her poster bed's duvet. She was wearing a sheer negligee, reading a romance novel, appearing to be completely helpless. Yet, at that moment, I felt like the one who might need help.

I was about to shut the door behind me before I was seen by any outside guards, when I stopped in my tracks at the sight of her. It was as if my legs had frozen inside the half-open doorway. I was mesmerized.

She glanced up from her book, as if I was someone she had been expecting. She calmly said, "Well, don't let all of the heat out." Then she returned her attention to her paperback, seemingly oblivious to the strange man who had just appeared in her bedroom. And she was no less concerned about her state of undress.

I closed the door, but didn't proceed any farther inside, doubting my next move.

It struck me that she must have thought I was someone else, who visited her bedroom often... Or maybe she was blind. Obviously stupid, because she was reading a book. While keeping my eyes on her, I tried to get a sense of her room, noticing another French door leading to an inside hallway. We were alone.

"Make yourself comfortable," she said tapping a spot beside her. "I want to finish this chapter." She didn't even look up as she said this.

She laughed at something she read, and then put her novel down. A sultry smile clung to her as delicately as her outfit did to her skin, and her eyes considered me from head to toe.

Without any doubt, she was the most beautiful woman I had set my eyes on.

"I'm Patsy. What do they call you in the mountains you come from?"

And funny too, I thought. But I had a job to do. "Where's your mother?" I huffed. After knocking the outside guard unconscious, I checked her mother's room downstairs. It was empty.

"I doubt she'll walk in on us, if that's what you're afraid of. C'mon over and take your clothes off."

I should have already tied her up at this point, rather than engaging her in her foreplay. Yet I couldn't stop. "You're not much on ceremony, are you?"

"Life's too short. Are we going to get to it, or what?" she asked.

Yeah, I laughed, but I didn't answer her. I generally avoided talking to anyone because there was too much of it going around. I always knew what to say, regardless of the situation. But for the first time in my life, I was utterly speechless.

She arched her back, sticking her chest out farther than it did naturally. Then she lifted her smile up higher and fluttered her eyelids playfully.

I wasn't sure if she was just playing me, or she was serious about her amorous intentions. But one thing I knew: Joey had no chance with this one. Patsy was way more woman than any man could handle... Any man, except maybe me.

Stick to the mission, I told myself.

I stepped closer, intending to tie her up and then go looking for her mother. I needed both for my plan to work. But I hesitated when I heard another woman's muffled protest coming from inside, followed by approaching footsteps.

"Don't be shy," Patsy continued from her bed. "I only bite where you'd like it."

Believe me when I say it was unbearably difficult to ignore this seductress. But I did by drilling my eyes on the interior door and the other woman's voice just behind it.

"I can walk on my own, thank you!" the voice behind the door insisted.

Patsy sat up and said rapid fire, "Well, don't I have all the luck. You better hide, before Mother comes in and finds us about to do the wet mamba."

I hesitated again, suppressing another laugh, before I dashed to her side of the bed and ducked down behind it, while pointing my gun at her.

She rolled her eyes. "I know—I know. If I say anything, you'll do something to me I won't like."

The door clicked open, and her head snapped in that direction. The door closed, and there was the distinctive sound of a lock engaging. I rose to a stand, with a forefinger to my lips, while still holding my rifle in Patsy's general direction. Of course, the safety was on.

"Hi Mama," Patsy said. "This is exactly as it looks. And this strange man was about to spank me for something I did wrong." Patsy rolled onto her knees and thrust out her rear end.

"Patsy, for the love of God, get some damned clothes on," demanded the woman, who looked like an older doppelgänger of Patsy. Her hands were on her hips and her brow furrowed. She was angry at her daughter, but not afraid of me or my weapon.

Once again, I was taken aback by the fact that not just one, but two women were completely unperturbed by my supposedly unexpected presence. "Both of you, put some clothes on," I whispered. "Were leaving right now."

"My coat is downstairs," said the woman to me. "Patsy, loan your mother one of your coats," she said to her daughter.

"Wilma McBoyd, at your service, Mr..." Wilma held out a small hand for me to shake.

"Compton. And this is the last time I'm going to ask" Would you please get dressed? We need to leave right now."

Patsy's expression changed from sultry to serious. She nodded and both women moved to a wardrobe where they put on winter clothing and fur coats.

When they were dressed and ready to go, I pulled out my remote control, held it up and pressed a button. A satisfying boom sounded outside.

"That's our cue," I said. "After you."

CHAPTER 22

Leticia

The guard pulled me away from the RV, leaving Dog locked up there. That was probably good, because I didn't want to see what Dog did to the other guard, who was no longer screaming in fear.

It was also good the guard who had a hold on me didn't have the guts to open the door. I was afraid he would use the opportunity to shoot Dog. It was better that Dog was where he was.

"The Halstons must be desperate if they're recruiting kids to do their dirty work," the out-of-breath guard huffed.

Then it occurred to me, I had failed my friends once again. Not only had I already lost our only way of finding our permanent home, and failed to retrieve them, I stupidly got Dog and me trapped. Still, I wasn't going to give up too easily.

The guard had hold of me by the sleeve of my jacket and pulled me toward the blockade, and I would presume a vehicle where he would drive me to see his superior. But when he slipped on an icy part of the snow, I reacted by swinging around and out of his grasp. I ran for it. Unfortunately, I encountered the same problem.

By a red spot—It's blood—I lost my footing and fell hard, face first. I wasn't sure what a concussion was supposed to feel like, but it couldn't have been much worse than this. I also understood what it was like to see stars.

A long period of time seemed to have passed, while I remained there, nonplussed, my face smushed into the ice pack. I was there long enough that I felt a warm wetness pool around my face. I'm bleeding. Then I heard a series of swear words and I felt the guard's heavy hand on my arm, tugging me back up.

He yanked at my other arm, bending it funny. Then there was a zipping sound... He zip-tied me!

I tried to move my arms and couldn't because they were secured behind my back. Even though my head clanged with pain, I smiled at this. I actually knew how to break out of zip ties because I read about this in one of my spy novels.

"You're not getting away from me now," the guard stated proudly.

I must have snickered, because in response, he jerked at my arms so hard, I thought they might pop out of my shoulders. I shrieked in pain and felt tears threaten, but I wouldn't have any of that. If I were Nan, I would have thought this was my punishment for what I had done to my friends. But like Nan, I still had fight in me. I had a few advantages over this guy. If I could remain calm, maybe I could get free and figure out where they had taken our stuff. Perhaps this guy would take me directly to where they were.

He had me up on my feet and moving forward, with him painfully steering me by my arms.

"I'm taking you to the boss. He don't take kindly to spies."

He called me a spy. I wasn't sure if I should be proud or scared. "Does Mr. McBoyd shoot spies?" I asked, trying to sound like I imagined secret spies would have sounded in my novels.

"I would imagine."

In one of my spy novels, the captive used his superior intellect to insult and confuse his captors so he could gain the upper hand. That should be easy with this one. "Didn't think you had any imagination," I said.

"You getting smart with me?" the guard asked through his teeth.

"That wouldn't be too hard," I quipped.

He lifted up on my arms, causing a sharp enough pain that I grunted. "Don't feel too good, do it?" he said. If I could see him, I'm sure he would have been smugly smiling at his efforts to cause me pain. Fight on!

We were headed toward a big truck nearby.

"So, what I'm curious about," I said, trying to act nonchalant, "is what Mr. McBoyd will do with you."

"Whaddya mean?" he said, slowing us a bit.

"Just that I wonder if your boss would like the fact that you had allowed one of his men to get eaten by my dog. And then left him to die, without trying to save him."

The guard stopped us.

I turned to see that the guard was eyeballing the RV's side entrance. I could almost smell the gears of his feeble mind grind to a halt. But then I started to panic. Because once again, this might cause him to release Dog and then shoot him.

"I'll just tell Boss, Chip was already dead and you closed the door on him. I had to run after you." He smiled at this. "Boss will believe me over a spy." He pushed me forward again.

"I'll bet your boss was excited when you found all of our stuff?"

"Oh man, was he. Especially the guns and ammo." He helped me into the back seat of the truck. Then he got into the driver's side and started up the truck.

"Bet the map was interesting too?" I asked, hoping he'd tell me something I could use.

He glowered at me. "Don't know what you mean. Boss and Scud grabbed other things and took them back to the house. Nuff talking."

He put the truck into gear and drove us not very far, over a bridge, to a small trail cut out of the snow. It wound around a hill and then connected to another road. Then finally, we were at a gate with several men standing in front of it. All had guns.

The guard rolled his window down and said, "Have a prisoner in back." He pointed a thumb in my direction and the guy he was talking to peeked in to see me. "Going to take her to the boss."

"All right, open up," the man hollered and made fanning motions to have us go through.

We passed through an old iron gate, with stylized lettering on it, which spelled out "McBoyd."

We were headed down a long drive. In the distance there was a stand of trees and a large home, where I hoped I would find our supplies. I didn't know how I would find them, much less get them back. I just knew I had to if I was to make up for my mistakes.

I was testing the strength of my bindings when I felt a percussive wave, followed by a boom. Then we were in the air.

CHAPTER 23

Ron

That must have been our diversion.

The explosion was really close. It shook the windows and walls of McBoyd's home.

Bobby slammed the mug he was drinking from down onto the table. Some sort of hot tea sloshed out and all over the map he'd been proudly showing us. He rushed out the front door, and so did the other two guards who were supposed to be keeping an eye on us. They forgot us entirely.

"Follow me," Joey whispered and he dashed in the other direction, past a sweeping staircase. We were almost out of the living room when Joey collided with one of McBoyd's men running in our direction.

The man bounced off Joey and was spun around. Realization hit: The man lifted his rifle, intending to point it at Joey and me, when Joey reacted with a fist to the man's throat, immediately followed by a right elbow to the man's face. Joey then drove his foot into the man's lower leg, sending him to the ground, where he struggled to breathe.

"You'll have to show me that move some day," I said. But he didn't wait to acknowledge.

"Come on," he said and continued through the kitchen. I followed, keeping aware for anyone else.

At a side door, Joey cracked it open. He poked his head through and then pulled it back. "Looks like a clear shot all the way to our rally point." He gave me a serious glare. "You ready?"

I nodded and we both darted out the door, racing side-by-side for the tree line.

It was maybe one hundred feet to safety, but when you're out in the open, it feels like a mile.

There was smoke and a fire out by the front entrance, and several men running in that direction. There didn't appear to be anyone around the back of the property or on our side. It was clear.

Once in the cover of trees, we searched for our packs and weapons, where we had last seen Compton. We found them, but not him. "You see Compton?" I asked Joey.

He shook his head. "No!"

Out came my binoculars from my backpack. "I'd like to get a look at the explosion. I'll also keep an eye out for anyone coming our way, if you'll check and see if Compton is at the snowmobile?"

Joey nodded. "If he's there, I'll come back and get you. If you see anyone coming this way, don't engage, just double back to the snowmobile."

"Sounds good," I said, while Joey checked his weapon and then dashed off into an opening in the snow-covered trees, barely making a sound.

Staying low, I crept back to the edge of the tree line. From there, I had a one-eighty-degree view of McBoyd's property, as the tree line shot from back to front in a straight line for close to a mile, before it turned to the left ninety degrees through McBoyd's private road.

One of his people dashed by, forcing me to duck down below a bush. The man headed to where black smoke rose into the sky.

With binoculars, I could see that the explosion was set off right in the middle of McBoyd's unpaved road, right at the tree line that crossed through it. The damage was substantial: The road was impassible and in front of it was a truck that must have driven over it at the explosion point.

With one explosion Compton did in fact divert McBoyd and his men's attention to the front of the property, away from us. And as an added bonus, he blocked the only route in or out of McBoyd's house. If we were at war with McBoyd, Compton's plan was brilliant.

But that wasn't the point of our mission, was it?

As I watched McBoyd's men work to get to the flipped-on-its-side truck that had been blown up in the middle of the drive, I considered our mission. The explosion, like much of what Compton did, was excessive. The whole point of Joey and me going directly to McBoyd's home unarmed was to talk and try to convince the man not to attack. Instead, Compton single-handedly declared our group as enemies, along with the Halstons, ensuring that Bobby McBoyd would attack.

Joey and I saw his plans. He was proud to show us how his twenty-five men would converge on the Halston property at first light and kill everyone. As Trunk had suspected, there would be no way to stop the carnage. McBoyd had the weapons and ammo—much of it supplied by us—and he had the overwhelming manpower. We might be able to kill one or two of McBoyd's men, but they would get us in the end.

I learned my lesson from El Oso Polar. When you are dealing with a force which is much greater than yours and they intend to take what is yours, your only route is to get out of their way and let them have it. That was what we had to do.

I jumped when someone tapped me on the shoulder. "Snowmobile's gone," Joey whispered in my ear. "I assume he headed back ahead of us, as he said he would."

My heart sank when Joey told me this, while I kept my eyes on McBoyd's men working on the truck. They just pulled out the driver and they were attempting to pull out a passenger in the back seat.

"I think we should head back on the trail on foot," Joey continued. "And hope that Compton does what he said and returns to pick us up. If not—What, do you see?"

I had held up a hand to quiet him because what I saw felt as bad as getting shot. I looked again and let my head drop forward.

"What do you see?" Joey pleaded, but still at a whisper.

I handed him my binoculars and he looked. "Is that Leticia?" he asked.

"I'm afraid so."

CHAPTER 24

Nan

"What was that?" I asked.

"I don't know," Suzie said, standing up in a patch of green, holding a basket of cucumbers that she'd just picked. "It sounded like an explosion, but farther away than on our property."

"Oh no," I said. "It's Compton. I know it." I ran for the door. We were in one of the far buildings, but I made for the doorway that led to the farthest exit. The other one was two buildings to the outside. But I didn't care to have to walk through the deep snow. Ultimately, this would be quicker.

"I'm coming with you," Susie said, leaving her basket of vegetables behind.

We were out of breath when we reached the Power Generation Building. We collected our coats there and we were zippered up by the time we reached its exit.

Outside, there was no sign of any explosion. But Halstons' property was still a buzz of activity.

"There," Susie said, pointing at the sky to our left.

It was an overcast day, as it seemed to be every day. Yet there was more visibility now than earlier, and way more than in previous days. In the distance, a mile or so away, there was some black smoke coming from the ground.

"I see it," I said. "Is that McBoyd's place?"

"Yes, I'm sure of it," she replied.

"I'm going to check on Chloe and Leticia, and make sure they're fine," I said, turning to that direction.

"If you see Trunk, can you send him this way?"

"Sure." I ran, but much more gingerly, as the surface of the walkway down seemed slicker than when we had come up it.

Is Ron safe? I wondered and felt pangs of worry build up in me. I trusted Compton more than Ron did. But Ron was not trained like Joey and Compton were. I just hoped he was okay and didn't do anything stupid to put himself in harm's way.

I put on my best smile as I entered the Halstons' home, and made my way to the room Chloe, Leticia and Dog were staying in. Leticia and Dog had walked back to check on Chloe hours ago but hadn't reported back. Leticia looked tired then, so I assumed that she had taken Dog to their room to catch up on their sleep after the trying time they had last night. So I was surprised when I only saw Chloe.

"Oh, thank God you're here, Nan," Chloe croaked in a weak voice. "I'm all alone, and no one will tell me what's going on."

"Hey, Chloe. You look great," I said, trying to sound truthful as I approached. I sat down beside her bed and felt her head. She was cool but looked a little pale. "Still, you should lie back down."

"Was that an explosion?" she asked.

Damn, she heard that too, I thought. Chloe didn't know anything about the threatened attack by the McBoyds: we'd agreed it wasn't good to upset her, at least until she was on the mend. But if the attack was indeed going to happen tomorrow, she had every right to know. She'd surely ask questions if we had to move her someplace safe without telling her why.

"Nan?" she begged, still sitting up. "Please tell me what's going on."

"Okay, but only if you lie back down," I insisted, nudging her back with a hand on her shoulder.

She did.

"I need you to remain calm. It's important for you and the baby." I smiled, even though I didn't like pretending. "So our hosts, the Halstons have a neighbor who hates them because of a multi-generational feud. And they have threatened to attack this place tomorrow, if the Halstons don't turn over their property."

Chloe popped back up to a sitting position. "Have they started the attack?" she said, almost immediately convulsing in heavy breaths.

"No. I believe that was Compton. Compton, Ron..." I hesitated, "...and Joey are there now." I squeezed her hand to try to reassure her (or me).

"Oh no. Are they okay?"

"I'm sure they are. I'm more worried about Ron. Your Joey can take care of himself, and I know Compton will protect them both."

"Your Ron... I mean Ron is very capable of taking care of himself too," she replied. And I couldn't help but smile at this, because it was nice to think of him as my Ron, even though he wasn't.

"What are we going to do?" she asked.

"I'm not sure, but we'll figure something out. We always do. Together."

She nodded with a smile and then a grimace as she lay back down.

I looked around the room again, eyeing Leticia's bed, next to Chloe's. "You have any idea where Leticia and Dog went?"

"No, they came in and checked on me. Then they left maybe an hour ago, maybe longer."

"Okay, well you sit tight and get more sleep. I'll update you as soon as I know something."

"Promise?"

"Yes, I promise," I said, letting go of her hand and fast-stepping it to the exit. I needed to find out what was going on and what the guys were up to.

When I entered the living room, I found Trunk headed outside and I ran to catch up to him. "Hey, Trunk. Do you know what that was?"

He put an arm around me, so we were walking in the same direction, toward the Fields, instead of his gate, where I expected him to be going. "Nan, hi. One of my men said it was an explosion at McBoyd's place. But we don't know if your friends caused it or if it was an accident. Did you have explosives?"

We did. But I wasn't sure if it was right to tell him this secret yet. Compton made it a point to tell us to never tell anyone about them. "I don't know. I would have thought I would have seen it if we did." That was a half lie, as I never saw inside the pack that Compton kept them in.

In the distance, a noise grew.

Zooming past the Fields, a snowmobile approached. It was the one that the men had left on earlier. It was coming right for us, following the same trail it had left on earlier.

We stopped just off the front corner of the house to await its arrival. As it got closer, I could better see three figures on it. I expected them to be Compton, Joey and Ron. But only Compton was recognizable. The other two were women.

Compton was driving, followed by a young black-haired woman with her arms wrapped tight around him. The other a carbon copy, only older, clutched the sides of the snowmobile.

Suzie had run down the path and was now waiting with us.

When Compton pulled up in front of us, they all dismounted.

"What in the Samuel Hill have you gone and done, Mr. Compton?" Trunk barked.

"I've taken hostages," Compton said. "And I've left a note informing McBoyd to call off the attack or I'd kill them."

The younger woman put an arm around Compton. "Ain't my man scary-sounding?" A sly smile shot up her face. "Oh, hi Mrs. H."

"Hi Patsy," Suzie responded. "Hi Wilma," she said this to the older woman, beside Patsy.

"Hey Suz," said Wilma. "Our men are sure causing a ruckus, ain't they?"

CHAPTER 25

Ron

"Where do you think you're going?" Joey asked me.

I turned to face him. "I'm going to get Leticia. Are you coming?"

I had no idea what we were going to do when we got there. I just knew that we couldn't leave her.

"Do you have a plan?" Joey asked.

"Nope. I'm open to one if you have one," I said.

"Let's go, get in and get out as fast as we can." Joey smiled, as he knew that's what I would say.

"Okay, let's go then."

We marched double-time toward the explosion site, following a diagonal path others had trod through the snow. Our heads were constantly turning, as if on a swivel, looking for anyone who might get in our way.

"Eleven o'clock," I said, calling his attention to someone running down the driveway toward the accident.

"Not a combatant," Joey said. "Let's keep on moving."

We arrived at the overturned truck, unobstructed. I passed by a red-headed kid with a rifle, who just looked at me, but didn't threaten.

Because we arrived on the other side of the explosion site, we missed that the explosion survivors were already being moved by stretcher. So we headed up the driveway toward the house, attempting to catch up with Leticia's stretcher. Still, no one bothered to stop us.

The driver was already being taken inside the house. Leticia was halfway there. So Joey and I followed from behind. Joey signaled that he would take the most forward stretcher guy and I would take the rear stretcher guy.

I nodded in agreement. I knew that Joey's actions would not only take out the lead guy but divert my target's attention. I had never been taught hand-to-hand combat like Joey, but I had been in a few street fights before. I just did not want to have to shoot the guy.

Leticia looked bloody and appeared to be unconscious. We needed to get her back to Suzie quick. I mouthed a prayer that Suzie said last night. "Lord, please look after us and help me do your bidding." I hoped the Lord's bidding and mine were the same.

Joey said something about keeping eyes on what's behind us. I looked back and then to him, and he gave me the thumbs up. He was just confirming that it was only us and the two carrying the stretcher. He dashed forward.

Without thinking, I took my rifle and swung it at the back of the rear stretcher-bearer's head. He lunged forward as Joey passed by him, causing his hold on the stretcher to drop.

The forward guy was pulled back when the other end of the stretcher dragged. He stopped and turned just as Joey hit him hard in the face with an elbow, knocking him to the ground.

The rear guy—my guy—turned to face me. Unfortunately, this guy was taller and heavier than me, and he looked pissed. He had one of my AR pistols around his neck, and he started to reach for it when I did what I saw Joey do earlier.

I lunged with my fist stiff like a hammer and drove this into the man's throat. In a blur to me, and him, I drove my left arm down on his arm, knocking his hand away from the gun's grip. Then I stomped on the man's knee, sending him to the ground, writhing in pain and gasping for air. It almost felt like someone else had just done this. Then I found that I was gasping for air too.

Joey had a bigger problem.

The forward stretcher-bearer had a knife out, whereas Joey had moved his rifle to his back. Joey unsheathed his knife and said to the guy, "You know, Scud, we don't have to do this. We just want the girl."

"Joe, you broke my Patsy's heart. I'm going to enjoy this," he said and then rushed Joey, with his knife raised in a stabbing motion. The man drove his knife down, but Joey was there, blocking with both arms. He deflected the man's stab and then instantly swung an elbow around, only grazing the man, but knocking him back off his stance.

"I told you, Scud, I don't want to hurt you," Joey pleaded. "You know Patsy doesn't even like me anymore."

"BS, she's mentioned your name twice today," Scud said, driving his knife at Joey's abdomen, his eyes wild with fury.

Joey reacted so quickly, I almost didn't see his movement.

He deflected and then punched Scud with the blunt end of the knife, drawing blood.

Scud, doubled back, staggering.

"Last warning, Scud," Joey offered. He wasn't even out of breath.

Scud grunted and then came at Joey like a locomotive, low and fast, holding the knife with both hands and yelling expletives at him. It almost looked like he would hit Joey, but at the last possible moment, Joey parried out of the way, while also driving his own knife into the Scud's leg. Scud collapsed to the ground, clutching at his wound.

I must have been standing there in awe because Joey said, "He'll live, I got muscle."

Darting back, I scooped up Leticia and broke for the woods.

Joey, right beside me, yelled back, "Tell Patsy I'm sorry. I will always love our time together, but I found someone else, and we're going to have a baby."

CHAPTER 26

Leticia

I woke up in Ronald's arms

I thought it was a dream, one that had played out in my mind many times before where Ronald pulled me out of a cauldron of fire and carried me to safety.

Then the icy cold bite at my face and a blinding headache wrestled me from the dream...

I was blown up!

I must have convulsed at this thought because Ronald's grip around me tightened. He tilted his face toward mine and he mouthed the words, "You're all right. I've got you, Leticia."

My imagination filled in the sounds that my ears weren't hearing. I guess when you get blown up, your ears don't work too well. I should have checked my limbs to make sure they were still there, but it was only at that moment that the remaining parts of this larger problem became obvious to me. "Dog!" I yelled.

Ronald slowed his movement more and I think I heard him say, "What about Dog?"

"I was so stupid. I went to the RV that the bad men took from us, because I had to get the map and logbook I left there—"

"Whoa-whoa. Slow down and tell me about Dog," he said.

Can I hear now or did I get really good at reading lips?

"Ronald, over here," Joey said from somewhere I couldn't see, confirming my answer.

"Dog is trapped," I said. "He attacked, and I think killed, a man inside the RV. But he's trapped inside. I'm afraid the bad men will kill him if we don't get to him first."

"Don't worry, Leticia. We'll get Dog. But first we have to get to the ranch," he said in his soothing voice.

"How is she?" Joey asked, right behind me.

"She's fine and will have a great story to tell her children someday," Ronald said.

The dream seemed broken then. I knew that it wouldn't be our children. He meant when I met someone one in the future and we had children, and my children read one of my books. But somehow, I didn't mind. I could still enjoy the dream, whenever I wanted.

"I know how to walk," I said, giving a firm push with my arm.

He stopped and lowered me into a well-trodden area of snow, overlooking a canyon of icicles. "Tell me how this feels," he said, always showing concern.

"I'm good. Shouldn't we be going back?" I asked and turned to face both Ronald and Joey.

Joey answered. "It doesn't look like anyone saw us. And Compton did say that we should head back on the trail if he was already gone."

I didn't know what he meant by trail, and I didn't think I really wanted to know, but his logic was good. "And you promised to get Dog before it's too late."

"Okay, let's double-time it then," Ronald instructed Joey. Then to me, "Leticia, if you can't keep up, we'll have to carry you."

I was about to answer that I could run circles around both of these old men, when they became alert, stepped around me and pointed their guns at some point down the canyon. I shrank down because I couldn't hear what they obviously heard.

Perhaps your hearing was damaged after all, I told myself.

Then I heard what sounded like a motor.

It looked like Compton driving some sort of giant snowmobile, although I think it could have been called a snow tank.

He passed us without looking, turned the snow tank around, and then stopped facing the place he had come from.

We were jogging to him before he'd stopped.

"Surprising what you pick up on this trail, huh?" he said, obviously trying to be humorous.

"Where have you been?" Ron demanded. He sounded pretty angry, but I didn't know why. Compton saved us a walk all the way to the ranch.

"I've been busy saving the world, again," Compton said. "Get on, we need to get out of here."

"Don't have to ask me twice," Joey said and he hopped on.

"You get on next," Ronald instructed me, “and I'll bring up the rear.”

"Hey Joey," Compton yelled as he gunned the engine. "Met your girlfriend."

I couldn't see Joey's face, but because I had my arms around him for support, I could feel him tense up. "What did you do?" he yelled.

"Don't get your panties in a knot. She's fine. Patsy and her mother are at Halston's place."

Compton moved us forward, and I guessed that that was the end of their conversation. Then he said, "Your girlfriend is quite a woman."

CHAPTER 27

Nan

Like a vivid memory, a phone's classic ringtone reverberated from the kitchen, demanding an answer.

Most of us had just come in from the outside, including the so-called hostages. After our quick introductions, Compton left immediately on the large snowmobile, minus the trailer, because he said it would "slow me down." When I had asked where Ron and Joey were, he said he was going back to retrieve them. He had expertly turned himself around and disappeared across the Halstons' upper open field. Trunk too left, after saying that he would be right back, and marched off around the house.

When what sounded like a phone rang, Suzie announced, "I haven't heard that phone ring since McBoyd had called to announce that we were the cause of his failing hot springs... I'll bet I can guess what he's calling about this time."

Several things occurred to me, all of them seemed odd: they had a landline and it was still working, when all public services had been down for months; McBoyd could have delivered his ultimatum by phone, but instead chose the more provocative method of delivering the dead body with a note; McBoyd had not used this phone since, but when his daughter and wife were abducted, he got right on the phone; and how did she know it was McBoyd calling and not someone else?

Suzie had quickly scooted to the kitchen, discarding her coat on a chair, to answer the ring-ring-ring of the phone. The rest of us shuffled in behind her. I heard Suzie answer, just before I saw her speaking on a red Slimline phone.

"Hello, this is Suzie," she said addressing the base where the curly phone cord connected to the wall. Her face was at first her typical warm and welcoming expression; a pleasant smile held for just a moment after her "Hello." But the smile quickly faded, and her face tightened.

We couldn't hear the words, but the other end was screaming.

"Yes Bobby, your wife and daughter are here."

More screaming.

"Yes, of course they're fine."

She cocked her head in a questioning manner.

"Sure, you can speak to her."

She put the receiver against her chest and turned to us. "Patsy, your father wants to speak to you."

Patsy stepped forward and took the phone. "Hi Daddy, how—"

Patsy held the phone away from her ear and then put it back.

"Yes, Daddy. As Mrs. H said, I'm fine."

She pulled the phone from her ear once more for just a moment, before responding. "No, it was a man named Compton. He—"

She pulled phone away, then smiled like a Cheshire Cat before answering.

"No, that brute of a man didn't hurt me, but only because Mama came in at the moment that he was going to ravage my bod—"

Her smirk turned into a questioning scowl.

"No, I have not seen Joey Macaroni. And yes, I still miss him, Daddy. Why?"

Her mouth opened, her eyes crossed, and she shook her head, like she had heard the most ridiculous thing.

"Whatever, Daddy."

She looked at us.

"Who?" she asked and then listened.

"No, but Mrs. H. is." She nodded.

"Okay, here's Mrs. H." She held out the phone, dangling it by its cord, waiting for Suzie to take it back.

The theater we were witnessing was both entertaining and instructional. It was obvious that Patsy was busy pushing her father's buttons, like she must have done when she was little, even though now she was probably thirty. And by my guess, everything she said was purposeful in generating the desired response she wanted from her father. But what that was, I didn't yet know.

Suzie grabbed the phone. "Yes, Bobby." This time her smile wasn't genuine.

What proceeded was an entirely one-sided conversation that went on for at least two minutes. Other than a few "mm-hmms" on her part, she said nothing. And because her expressions were stoic, there was no way to tell how the conversation was going. Finally, she hung up unceremoniously, without a "goodbye."

Suzie, at least I thought, was looking at us for some feedback. But then I realized Trunk had quietly returned and was now behind us. He said, "Well, what did that old windbag have to say?"

Suzie cleared her throat. "In a nutshell, Bobby McBoyd said that the terms of his ultimatum have changed. If we return Wilma and Patsy back to him unharmed, and Patsy and Joey are immediately married by you, he'll postpone the planned attack tomorrow. However, if the women aren't returned or the wedding doesn't take place by tomorrow, he'll attack."

Two more things struck me at that moment. First, Bobby McBoyd sounded batshit crazy, and second, I was glad Chloe was in bed and didn't hear any of this.

CHAPTER 28

Ron

We arrived back at Halstons' property, but there was no one there to greet us. It was uncomfortably cold outside—but when wasn't it these days—so it shouldn't have been a surprise that everyone would be inside.

I was looking for Suzie, so she could give Leticia the once-over. Leticia appeared to have had only been scratched up and sustained no serious injuries. But I was concerned she might have a concussion, or that I had missed something else. Concussions were bad things and I wanted to confirm she was fine fairly quickly.

Upon entering the Halston living room, we found Suzie and Trunk Halston, his older brother George, who lived on the ranch, along with Nan and two other women I had not met yet. But when Joey grunted beside me and I saw him rustle uncomfortably, I figured there was more to this than I knew.

The room had gone quiet when we entered, and Suzie immediately popped up from her seat upon seeing us. "Leticia, honey, are you all right?" She marched right over to get a closer look.

"She was in the truck that was blown up." I turned to glare at Compton and continued, "We're hoping you can confirm it's nothing but a few scratches."

Compton ignored me and watched Suzie sit Leticia down on a chair and ask her questions, while holding up a forefinger in front of her eyes.

George Halston had been saying something that sounded positive about the McBoyds, with his back up against the bookshelves in the corner of the living room. Until now, I had not seen George for more than a second. Now, seeing more of him and Trunk together, I noticed the differences: Trunk was a strong man with strong convictions, while at the same time a pacifist; George struck me as a weak man, like Bigelow. And also, like Bigelow, George seemed afraid. It was something Compton warned me about how fearful men were dangerous in these times, because they often made poor decisions.

"Guess I should introduce our... guests," Trunk said, rising from his seat, as did the two women. "Compton and Joey are already familiar... Ron, this is Bobby McBoyd's wife, Wilma McBoyd and her daughter, Patsy McBoyd."

"Also known as the jilted fiancée," the younger of the two stated, and then curtsied while giggling.

I was more taken aback by the two of them: They could have been twin sisters, seemingly not separated by much more than a decade in age.

"And guests is sort of a loose term," Wilma said. "In most circles, we would be called hostages. Although I don't blame Trunk and Suzie, who have been good hosts, as always."

At that moment, it all made sense: Compton's mission that he wouldn't tell us about was to take McBoyd's wife and daughter hostage to stop the attacks. This exchange also explained Joey's obvious embarrassment at being reunited with his ex-fiancé, Patsy.

"Hey Patsy," Joey said, his voice just a shade over a whisper.

"Hey yourself," Patsy shot back with a giddy smile.

"So how was this supposed to work?" I asked Compton.

Compton put his bag down and looked over at Patsy, who winked back at him. This part was also very curious.

"Something had to be done. There is no way to protect this place against McBoyd's overwhelming firepower and manpower. Short of a surprise attack, where we might get a few more of them than if we waited for them to attack, this was the only viable option."

"But we don't kidnap people!" Trunk stated, almost yelling. He took a breath and said, a little more calmly, "It's just not who we are."

"Shouldn't you tell them about father's most recent ultimatum?" Patsy said with a snicker.

Another curious detail: How would McBoyd have sent a message over, while he was busy with us escaping and blowing up a truck on his property?

"He said..." Trunk glanced at each of us. "If we return Wilma and Patsy to him unharmed and..." He hesitated, while scrutinizing Joey. "And if Patsy marries Joey, he'll stop the atta—"

"What?" Chloe cried out from the hallway, obviously listening. "You're going to marry your ex-fiancée?" The pitch of her voice could have broken glass. She turned and dashed away.

"Oh-oh," Patsy said, exaggerating her "oh's" with fully pursed lips, rounded like a zero. "Lucy, you got some 'splaining to doooo." It was a perfect mimic of the famous Desi Arnaz line when Lucille Ball did something wrong.

"Chloe, wait!" Joey hollered. "That's not going to happen." He ran after her. Halfway down the hallway a door slammed shut.

"And what did you tell him in response?" Compton asked.

"Nothing. Yet," Trunk said. "But I plan to tell him that I never agreed to kidnapping his wife and daughter; that this was just a big misunderstanding, perpetrated by a friend who meant well, while trying to stop violence."

Trunk offered Compton a friendly smile. "And I'm going to tell him that I'm having you return them for me, without conditions."

Compton let his head tilt forward and sighed. "Are you sure that's what you want to do?"

"Yes, I am," Trunk said to Compton. And then to us, "And of course, I'm not going to marry Joey and Patsy."

"Guess that leaves me open for other offers," Patsy said.

Compton looked over to Patsy, who once again offered him a wink, followed by a sultry smile. Then, I swear, Compton had to repress his own grin before returning his attention to Trunk.

Even though their lives hinged on the whims of a madman, it seemed like no one, except me, was taking this thing seriously enough.

"No," Compton said to Trunk. "What I meant is, does it make sense to give away your only bargaining chips, regardless of how you got them, and even though we all know that we were never going to ever harm them?"

"I'm sorry, but I just don't roll that way, Compton."

"Okay, fine," Compton said. "But what will you do when he says he's going to attack because you didn't marry Joey and Patsy as he demanded, or... when he shoots back with whatever other cockamamie ultimatum he comes up with then?"

I wondered this as well. As brash as Compton's plan was to kidnap the two women and use them to broker some sort of ceasefire, returning them without conditions didn't seem like the best option.

"I honestly don't know, Compton. But I do know that God will help us find a way out of this. He will lead us to an answer, and one without violence."

Trunk then did something I didn't expect. He gently grabbed the hand of his brother, who was standing beside him. "Pray with me, brother?" He looked up and added, "You're all welcome to stay and pray with us."

CHAPTER 29

Nan

Trunk marched over to the same kitchen phone his wife had used earlier to deliver his answer to McBoyd's ultimatum. Since Compton was to be part of that interchange and said he would update each of us, I left to check in on Leticia, Joey and Chloe. But Ron stopped me in the hallway, looking like he was about to deliver his own ultimatum.

He softly took my hand in his and gazed into my eyes.

I won't lie to you. At that moment, even though it would have seemed out of left field, I thought he was going to bend a knee and propose marriage. But there was an entirely different reason for his seriousness.

He leaned in and whispered into my ear, "Make sure everyone is packed up and ready to go when we return from dropping off the two women."

"Oh," I said, a bit startled by his decision on behalf of the group, not to mention where my mind had gone to. What he said was the right decision, but it stung a bit that he didn't even consult us before making it. "Where do you suggest we go?"

"I don't know. As Leticia pointed out, McBoyd has all the details of our Wyoming destination. So we can't go there. Maybe Bigelow's Colorado bunker. Regardless, we do know this thing is not going to work when your grand plan to save your ranch from a crazy, vengeful man rests on a prayer that 'God will provide an answer.' Plus, I saw McBoyd's plans. He really does intend to murder everyone and take everything... I just think we need to leave immediately."

"Okay, but what will Compton say?"

He kept his eyes locked on mine. "I figure we'll tell him as a group... Once I return with Dog."

He released me and then began the process of getting ready for the outside, putting on his coat over his AR pistol, which was perpetually slung under his arm.

"Wait, so where is Dog?" Until he said it, I hadn't even realized Dog was gone.

He hesitated before answering, rapid-fire. "Leticia had gone out to the RV to retrieve our stolen map, notes and the radio. That's how she ended up in a truck that was blown up by Compton's diversion."

He must have seen my reaction to this. "Yes, I know. Anyway, she said that Dog is trapped in the RV. I want to get him before McBoyd sends someone there who will have to hurt him to regain access to the RV. I should be back before the... ah, prisoner drop-off."

My head was spinning, and I didn't want him to go. But he was going to no matter how much I said this mission of his was filled with peril.

"Promise you'll play it safe?" I asked and then kissed his cheek.

"Promise," he said, offering me a natural smile.

I watched him exit before heading to Chloe's room. Now, besides needing to see how they were, there was news to deliver.

Chloe was sitting on the edge of her bed, wiping away tears, Joey beside her, speaking to her quietly. Leticia was on another bed on the other side of the room from them, perhaps giving Joey and Chloe some privacy. Suzie was sitting in a chair opposite her, applying a bandage to Letitia's head. Her other cuts appeared to have been already cleaned up.

"How's our intrepid patient doing?" I asked Suzie, while offering Leticia a big grin. She returned a forced grin of her own.

"Surprisingly well, considering..."

"I messed up everything, Nan." She flashed her sullen eyes downward before looking back up at me. "I lost the map and radio, then I lost Dog, then I got blown up..."

"You'll have lots to write about. You're just lucky you weren't hurt worse."

"Nah. Our mutual hero, Ronald, saved me. And so did—Hey, thanks Joey," she said, fixing her gaze up and past me.

"'Twas nuttin'," Joey answered in his usual warm twang, from behind me. "Speaking of which, where is our mutual hero, Ronald Ash?"

Suzie stood up. "I'll leave you in good hands then. Besides I want to see if Trunk has made contact with our friendly neighbors yet."

"He was just about to call Bobby McBoyd when I came back to check on this one," I said.

"Thanks, hun," Suzie said and marched out the door, shutting it behind her.

I waited until the door clicked closed before I spoke. "Okay, I just spoke to Ron, before he left. He said that we should all pack our bags. The thinking is that we should leave sometime after they deliver the McBoyd women back to Bobby, but certainly before tomorrow. So we should be ready to leave at a moment's notice."

"But we can't go to Blackstone without my map and book, and possibly the radio," Leticia said, while standing up. Her face was a twist of lines.

"He said we'd figure that part out together. But it is not safe here, where an inevitable war is about to break out."

"What does Compton think about this?" Joey asked.

"Ron hasn't asked Compton yet. He figured if we were unified on this, Compton would either choose to squeeze in with all of us or he'd stick around here."

"Perhaps we could go to Bigelow's millionaire bunker in Colorado," said Chloe, coming up beside Joey. "He keeps saying there is room for all of us."

Joey turned to Chloe, probably to give her a scolding look for getting back out of bed when she should have been resting... Even though now that would be impossible when we left.

He turned back to me. "You said you spoke to Ron, before he left. Where was he going?"

"Well..." I said. "He's going to the RV to go collect Dog."

"Oh no," Joey stated, looking agitated. "McBoyd said when we were there that he was planning on sending at least another guard out there to protect that line. That guard would already be there by now. So Ron may be walking right into trouble." Joey turned to go. "Alone." He kissed Chloe and then rushed out the door, saying, "Excuse me," before he disappeared.

I knew I should have done something to stop Ron from going.

There was a clatter behind me, and I turned to see Bigelow at the open door. Suzie had said that she'd given him a whole Xanax because he was in another full-on anxiety attack about hearing about McBoyd's threat. She had put him to bed, but that must not have lasted long. His hair was standing on end, and he yawned. "Hey, what did I miss?"

CHAPTER 30

Ron

I found myself once again walking alone in the cold, planning to do something incredibly stupid but absolutely necessary.

Getting Dog was not a question; it was an absolute. He saved my butt and those of my friends more times than I could count. I literaterly owed him my life. So of course, I was going. Then after I had left, my mind started needling me about not getting help from Joey, Compton, or even one of Trunk's men.

But everyone had others on their mind, and this was my dog. Besides, I was counting on a little luck: that none of McBoyd's men would have returned to the RV because of the chaos that Compton had created. But I needed to move quick. At some point soon, McBoyd's men would move forward, in preparation for Compton's delivery of the two women. And no doubt, it was going to take place on this very road.

The more I thought about what I might find, the quicker I moved, until I was jogging. When I came up to Halstons' road blockade, I slowed back to a walk.

"Halt," yelled a young guard, pointing his rifle in my direction.

My hands shot up into the air and I yelled back, "I'm Ronald Ash. My friends and I are staying with the Halstons."

It appeared that he hadn't heard my words, because he still had his rifle pointed at me. He was kneeling, using the bumper of a frozen car as his shield. He was still quite exposed, and to a trained shooter—which was not me—he would be easy to pick off...

Just one more reason not to hang around this place when the shooting starts.

He yelled, "Halt!" once more, his pitch even higher than his last warning.

"I'm a friend. I'm Ronald Ash. I'm staying with the Halstons. Please don't shoot." I was getting ready to hit the ground when finally, the young guard stood erect and lowered his weapon.

"What in tarnation are you doing walking around here?" his voice warbled. "Don't you know we're at war?"

Standing belly to belly with the man—a kid really, who didn't look old enough to shave—it occurred to me that it was often the old people of any organization that enlisted their young to die on the front lines of their wars. That's the way the world seemed to work, even after the apocalypse. But I wasn't going to be party to this war. We were leaving before the bullets started flying. After I got Dog.

"I'm headed to McBoyd's blockade. Our RV is stuck there, and so is my dog. I'm getting my dog."

The kid glared at me, either unable or unwilling to speak.

I continued. "So don't shoot me when I return in a few minutes, okay?"

At first, he didn't answer. So I stepped around the kid and made for the opening in the blockade of cars.

"You can't go there. I have orders to stop any one from going farther," the kid huffed in his shaky voice.

"That's to keep the enemy from coming this way. We've already established I'm not the enemy and that I'm going the other direction—that is, until I return. Okay?"

The kid played with his rifle, lifting it slightly. "Ah, I don't think I should let you go."

I was done with this conversation. "Still, I'm going. If you want to shoot one of Trunk Halston's guests, you go right ahead. I'll be returning in a few minutes with my dog."

This time I didn't wait for an answer. I marched off, slowly at first, but then returned to a jog within seconds. My need to get to the RV felt immediate.

Moments later, I was there, and I could hear Dog barking from the RV. Unfortunately, we weren't the only two there.

Nan

"War? What do you mean there's going to be a war?" Bigelow demanded.

This was in response to Leticia's adept synopsis of the problem we were facing with McBoyd.

Without answering, I put an arm on Bigelow's shoulder and steered him out of the room. Leticia was left with instructions to pack up her and Chloe's backpacks, and then to make sure Chloe rested until one of us brought word to get moving.

Bigelow persisted, peppering me with his annoying questions, as I led him through the hallway to the living room. "What are you going to do about this? How are you going to keep me safe? After all I did for your people, how could you get me into this mess? If I were—"

That's when I cut him off. "Enough! You are the most self-centered person I have ever met. You never would have made it this long without us. You would have starved to death in that mega-mansion of yours long ago. So don't bark at me. We could have just left your wimpy ass on the road to fend for yourself, but we didn't. So just stop."

Bigelow opened his mouth to spit out another useless argument about how we still owed him, when I spoke before he could. "What are you going to do? Sue us? If you haven't figured this out yet, we are living through Perdition now. We are paying now for all our sins, and buddy, I'll wager you have committed more sins than all of us combined. So maybe you're the cause of our problems and we'd be better off leaving you behind. Now leave me alone."

I stormed off, leaving him dumbfounded and sad. I felt both vindicated and depressed at what I said.

Then I found myself going from the frying pan into the fire.

Compton was animated, while standing up and making a point to Trunk, Suzie and the McBoyd women, when he saw me—and no doubt heard me—as I walked into the living room. "Nan... I was just about to ask if you had seen Joey. I want him to accompany me to the prisoner drop-off."

"Oh, honey," Patsy said from the couch, reaching up to touch Compton on his rear, "I'll be your prisoner anytime. I even have the handcu—"

Slap!

"Dammit, Patsy," Wilma said, withdrawing her hand from Patsy's face. "This is serious. You need to deal with reality for once."

Patsy's mouth was frozen open in a stunned scowl. She turned her scowl on her mother. "Look, Mother. The only one here who is not dealing with reality is you. You are the one who won't face the fact that my father is insane. He is the reason I'm thirty and still living at home. He's killed one of my boyfriends and drove off the only other man I loved. And now your husband threatens to murder these good people if I don't marry my old flame. And you say I'm not taking this seriously?"

She stood up and gave a tender look to Compton. "So what if I'm flirting with this man? At least he's a real man, who is set in his convictions. He's loyal and takes care of his people. And he doesn't murder." She smiled, and said softly, "I'd be with him if he asked me, because in the short time I've watched this man, behind his tough exterior, I know exists someone who is moral and kind." She turned to her mother. "What's your excuse?"

Before Wilma could answer, I had already walked around this unfolding soap opera, and made my way to the kitchen via the dining room. The physical connection between Patsy and Compton would have been the most interesting thing in my world, before our world ended and people were always trying to kill us. But Patsy's comments only reminded me further of how perilous our position was at Trunk and Suzie's ranch. Our welfare was dependent upon the whims of one mad man, and both his wife and daughter knew he was crazy.

Suzie kept a jug of fresh water in the kitchen and I was thirsty. So that was my target, while I waited anxiously for Ron and Joey's return, and hopefully shortly after that, our exit out of this craziness. I was about to push the door in and step through the kitchen doorway, when I heard and then caught a glimpse of Trunk's brother George. When I saw and heard what he was doing, I stepped back, hoping he hadn't seen me.

He was on the same phone that Suzie and Trunk had been using to communicate with Bobby McBoyd. Suzie later told me that the line still worked between their two places, but nowhere else outside of this.

In whispered tones, George spoke while eyeing the doorway I had been about to walk through.

"Yes, Sir," George said. "My brother Trunk planned the whole kidnapping. More importantly, he plans to ambush you and your people at the prisoner drop—" The phone clanged.

I sucked in a breath and took a step back.

The door flapped inward, and George stepped out, his gun pointed at me. "Not so fast," he said to me.

CHAPTER 31

Ron

Its movement was blindingly quick—a brown blur, streaking across the white, seemingly headed right for the RV and Dog's muffled woof.

When the blur stopped at the RV's door, it was recognizable. Millie, the McBoyd's German Shepherd that almost knocked Joey down at their door. Dog woofed in response.

They are speaking to each other.

It shouldn't be possible, but Dog often did the impossible. And now, somehow, McBoyd's dog was trying to free my dog from his RV confinement. But even for a hundred-plus-pound German Shepherd, this wasn't going to be that easy.

While keeping focused on this, I slipped through the blockade opening, clinging to an old 1980s Bronco. Also mesmerized by this display was an armed guard. He appeared from the other side when I almost bumped into him. At that moment, I froze, while he continued stepping forward, unaware of my presence, but only inches away from me.

My coat was zipped up over my AR pistol to keep its mechanisms and me from freezing up. There was no way to unzip and release my weapon without alerting him.

"Hey Millie, what are you doing here?" the man shouted, while he was rubbing his arms for warmth. His rifle was slung over his chest, under his arms.

I tried to shrink down lower, keeping my eyes glued on the man directly in front of me, and Millie barking about a hundred feet away.

The man spun around and brought his own rifle up. "Whoa! Where'd you come from? Hands up."

"Shit," I said under my breath, while sticking my hands into the air.

"You know I have orders to shoot any Halston that shows up here," said the red-headed guard, who looked real young, like he was still in high school.

Millie was scratching at the door, and I could hear Dog's thumping on the other side.

"I'm not a Halston. I'm Ron Ash. My friends and I were just visiting. We're not part of your war."

"Well then, what are you doing here?"

"It's Smittie, right? I came here to get my dog, then we're out of here."

He glowered at me, no doubt disquieted by my knowing his name. Then a rush of recognition hit him. "You were there with Joey Rancone and my uncle Bobby was showing you his plans."

Millie almost had the door. It was like she had figured out that the door's lever handle could be moved if she pushed down on it with both her paws. For all I knew, Dog told her from the other side of the door.

I looked back at the kid. "That's right. You saw we weren't armed, just like I'm not now. As I said, I'm only here to get my dog, who's locked in the RV. Which was our RV by the way, until your uncle shot it up."

Smittie had put some distance between me and him, but his rifle was pointed down. Although he was young, the kid seemed to have some presence of mind. He quietly considered what I said.

It was then that Millie got it. In one leap, she pushed down on the door handle while Dog pushed from behind, and the door flew open.

Dog sprang out and Millie barked her joy. Dog rubbed up against her and she against him. Perhaps it was dog-speak for thanks or nice to make your acquaintance. Then Dog saw me, and he yipped.

"Hi, Dog," I hollered.

He barked rapid-fire and dashed toward us.

"Halt," yelled Smittie. He lifted his rifle at Dog, who had already cut the distance between us in half.

"Don't. He's mine."

"If he doesn't stop, I'm going to fire."

"Dog, stop," I yelled, but it was no use; he wasn't stopping.

Bang!

Nan

"I didn't hear anything you were saying," I said. This came out dumb, as I was admitting that I knew that he said something he shouldn't.

"Right," George huffed. "My guess is you heard enough." I took a step back, wanting to get closer to the living room. "Freeze, or I will shoot you. Then I'll make up a story about how you tried to kill me. Who would my brother believe, some stranger or his brother?"

He took another step closer to me, pressing his pistol right against my gut. His finger was wrapped around the trigger. I could hear Bigelow and Compton getting into it. They felt miles away.

"In fact, turn around. I'm going to tell Trunk that you and your group were planning to steal our supplies... I said turn arou—"

Suz had just come in from the living room. "What do you mean you're going to tell your brother that these people were going to steal from us? And why do you have a gun on—"

"Shut up," George yelled. "Damn-damn-damn. You're always spoiling things for me, little Suzie-two-shoes. Go on, we're all going into the living room."

George had me turned with my back to him and my hands up, so my eyes were on Suzie. George jammed me in the small of my back and said, "Get moving."

The living room was silent, and all eyes were on Suzie and then me as I entered. George continued to roughly nudge me forward from behind.

"George, what in God's name has gotten into you?" Trunk asked, more animated than ever.

"Sit down and shut up, Brother," George said.

"Oh my Lord, he's got a gun," Bigelow squealed and dropped to the floor. Trunk sat down hard on the sofa. Patsy took the other, next to Wilma.

"You two sit down too, and I'll tell you a story," George said, while giving me another push with his pistol.

I trotted away and joined Suzie on two of the other chairs.

George waved the pistol at all of us. "Several years ago, my younger brother took control of our families lands, even though I was the eldest. Father always favored Trunk, from when we were kids. So even though this was my birthright, father gave everything to my brother, and I was left to become my brother's slave—"

"Wait a minute," Trunk said, standing up with a finger in the air.

"I said sit down," George hollered, pointing his pistol directly at Trunk, who then sat back in his seat. "It's my turn to tell you what to do, or so help me...

"So while McBride was suffering because his hot springs stopped, I offered him a way to get his cake and eat it too: We share the hot springs and the land, but he has to kill you."

"George Halston, how could you do that to your own brother?" Suzie barked.

"Right, Suzie-two-shoes. Go ahead and sit there in judgment over all of us sinners. Only I'm the one who now sits in judgment of y—"

His movements were so quick, it was over in an instant. Compton, who all of us had forgotten about, somehow snuck up on George and bashed him in the head, crumpling him to the floor.

Ron

"No!" I yelled, sure Smittie's bullet had struck Dog.

But Dog kept racing forward, taking one last bound before he leapt up at me, knocking me down to the ground. He happily slobbered all over my face, moaning his excitement as I felt his body for a wound.

He was fine.

I turned to look over at Smittie, who was rubbing his hands. His rifle lay at his feet. Beside him was Joey, pointing his weapon at Smittie.

"What happened?" I asked, while ruffling Dog's coat.

"Looks like I came along just in time. This guy was about to shoot Dog. I clobbered his hands, thankfully sending his bullet off the mark."

"I'm sorry, Ron," Smittie said. "I thought he was going to attack me."

I ignored the kid and turned to Joey. "Thank you for coming!"

"What the hell were you thinking doing this alone?" Joey said, walking over to hand me Smittie's rifle.

"I wasn't. And I was wrong. Thanks," I said.

Dog stepped away from me and barked at Millie, who woofed back and then trotted over to us.

"What's Millie doing here?" Joey asked.

"She released Dog from the RV."

Millie and Dog rubbed up against each other.

"Okay, she can come too, Dog," I told him.

"What do we do about him?" Joey asked.

"We'll take him back and then return him with the ladies."

CHAPTER 32

Leticia

I had the same dream I've usually had. Only this time, Ronald died.

My imagination always wove together dreamland fantasies of epic proportions, often involving two warring factions and me in the middle. In the end, my Sir Lancelot, my knight, Ronald Ash, would arrive at the last moment, when all hope was gone, and save me, his Guinevere. Every time, he would come away unscathed by the enemy's arrows or swords or spears, and he'd take me to my forever home, where we'd live happily ever after. This time, he couldn't avoid the arrows, and I watched him bleed to death.

I woke from this dream feeling a deep depression I hadn't felt since my parents were murdered. An inescapable feeling of despair lingered long after the images from my dream-turned-nightmare faded from the sleepy fog of my memory.

My parents had taught me to battle my emotions with logic. And this often worked. They said that conditions such as depression were often rooted in your feeling unable to control the events around you. Using logic and reason helped me to find the actions I had needed to take to push away any feelings of despair. It worked great.

That was, until they died.

It was then that I had come to understand that I had little control over the world around me, and that logic wasn't the answer. It was more like a salve to make you feel better. Logic never changed the facts: People were powerless, especially to those who were stronger than them.

Finding Ronald and Nan and the others helped me to live with this realization. After my parents' murder, and before Ronald and his friends saved me, I didn't want to live any more. Their presence and love didn't change the facts: There were always going to be elements and people I had no control over. But because of them, I was able to at least deal with the inexplicable feelings of dread, which were so common to me now. And when that didn't work, when it was too hard to deal with this world, I found it easy to escape to another one of my own making.

In my fantasy world, I had total control over everything. Even when my mind attempted to blend my conscious worries into my dream's narrative, I somehow was able to wrestle back control. And that was why Ronald was always the victor in my dreams and I always lived happily ever after. Until today.

After waking, the overwhelming melancholy from watching Ronald succumb to death still clung to me and wouldn't let go. From my bed, I glanced at Nan, hoping to go to her for a needed shot of strength. But she was still sleeping and so was Chloe.

Dog wagged his tail, sitting up, while gazing at me expectantly. He must have been waiting for me to wake. Like Ronald, he was always there, ready to save me. Maybe he was the Sir Lancelot I needed now.

"Hi Dog," I whispered, petting his head. "You're back," I said much too loudly.

A rather sizable, female German Shepherd was sitting next to Dog. She too was staring at me and wagging a tail. "Who's this... Is this your friend?" I asked, petting the Shepherd with my other hand.

Dog whimpered and then trotted off, the Shepherd following close behind.

What has happened while I was asleep? I wondered.

Then I remembered. I was half in a dream when I heard Ronald speaking to Nan, telling her that he was fine, that he and Joey had just returned after successfully retrieving Dog, and "a few other guests." The Shepherd must have been one of the "guests" he had spoken of.

Then I thought of Ronald and my dream... Is something bad going to happen to Ronald today?

Everyone was still asleep. So I got dressed and put my sleep clothes in my pack and went to the Halstons' library of books.

No one else was up, so I took some time to peruse all the books there. It wasn't that I felt much like reading. But I thought this activity might get my mind off my feelings of malaise. They had quite an eclectic collection: From Louis L'Amour paperbacks to science books—my favorite—to prepper books, to... My eyes halted on a series of Christian tomes.

I digested the titles and sub-titles of each book, some very small and some thicker than an inch. I pulled a dog-eared paperback that looked like it had been read quite a bit and took it back to our room.

I didn't read it right away. Instead, it sat on my lap, as I willed the weak light of the sun to begin coming through the windows, so that Chloe and Nan would wake up, and they could give me a dose of needed strength. Each long second that ticked away while waiting for them to wake filled me with more anxiety and the anticipation of the impending disaster I felt sure was coming today. None of us had any control over this.

My depression grew so untenable that my breathing started to hurt. I felt desperation for help. Any help. Then I remembered what Mrs. Halston and the book in my lap suggested.

Although the whole thing was foreign to me, I was ready to try anything... Even if it meant grasping for the divine.

I intertwined the fingers of my hands, tilted my head down and prayed.

Nan

Before sleep had taken me, I was warmed by feelings of joy and hope for the future, no matter how illogical that might have seemed at the time. When I awoke, those feelings were replaced by an overwhelming dread. In the moments before I got up, I tried to get my arms around this affliction.

Fear was a logical emotion with the unknowns that lay ahead. After what they were calling the prisoner drop-off, we were all leaving to an unknown place. And considering our world was controlled by evil people who proclaimed an exclusive license to take what they desired and murder whomever they wanted, it would be natural to fear what lay ahead. But fear was the norm now. It was as common as not seeing daylight in the middle of the day or seeing snow in the middle of summer. And until now, I had always felt that with Ron and our little family—which felt as strong as ever—we could tackle whatever punishment Perdition, as Suzie called it, threw at us.

That was until this moment.

Something horrible was coming. I felt it in my gut.

A peek through the window seemed to confirm this: The clouds were once again ominous and black, as they were in those early days of this icy apocalypse. An invisible wind howled outside, like an evil apparition called up from Hell's depths, noisily lamenting at its inability to pry its way through the house's weakest clapboards.

I resisted the need to arise, choosing instead to stay in my warm bed, with those whom I knew and loved still safe and close by, even if for just a moment longer. But If my feelings were correct, darkness was going to have its day today. And all of those I cared about would have to deal with the consequences. I guessed it was time to face the inevitable.

"Is it time?" Leticia asked across the room, obviously seeing I was awake.

It seemed like Chloe and Leticia stirred at once.

"What can I do, Nan?" asked Chloe.

"Me too," Leticia said, already dressed and ready to go, her backpack stuffed and zipped up. She got up, laid down a book she must have been reading, and sat beside me on my bed, wrapping her arms around my trunk.

She feels it too.

"I'm afraid there's not much we can do but wait for them to return from the drop off."

Was it better pushing forward the drop off until this morning? Compton said it was the tactically sound thing to do because it was too late yesterday to see anything. Mr. McBoyd agreed, but said that he would delay his attack no longer than Noon. Trunk said God would provide the answer before then. Ron told him we weren't going to wait for God: we were leaving after the drop off.

"It looks ugly out there, doesn't it?" Leticia asked, jostling me from my thoughts. She was gazing out through the window across the room. When the wind rattled the window frame, she squeezed tighter.

"Yes, it does."

We all looked up when Ron was at the door. "It's time for us to go."

Ron

Just as a gust of wind blew a curtain of white over our windshield, a strong feeling of foreboding struck me. There was no way to know why at the time.

Per Compton's demand, I was driving the Landcruiser for the prisoner drop, while he was riding shotgun. The two McBoyd women and McBoyd's nephew Smittie were in the back seat. Millie, the McBoyds' dog and George Halston—who was an interesting last-minute addition—were in the jump seat. When we were loading the so-called prisoners and Millie, Trunk brought out his brother George and announced to us, "Tell McBoyd if he likes my traitor brother so much, he can have him."

Compton had given me explicit orders to follow his lead this time, including shooting whomever I was told to. I may have been driving, but Compton was completely in charge of this mission. And although ceding control to someone else often gave me pause, this wasn't the reason for my misgivings. It was something else entirely.

The feeling was there after I woke from my recurring nightmare about Liz. It got worse when Nan and the others saw us off. Nan seemed especially gloomy about this mission. With tear-filled eyes, she pleaded with me to be careful. She said she was sure something bad was coming our way, but she couldn't explain why, only saying that it was a feeling.

I had gotten used to hearing Nan speaking about her bad feelings since we left our home several months ago. I couldn't blame her, after all the shit she'd gone through. I didn't know many people who could come out of what she experienced without becoming bitter and angry. Thankfully, she never let those emotions take possession of her. She was always hopeful, no matter what came at us, even with her anxieties.

Her strength was commendable, as it seemed every day we were faced with a new trial and tribulation. Once, after we had all consumed a little too much whiskey from a bottle we'd been saving, she admitted that she felt that many of our trials were her fault, because of the sins she had committed in the past.

I tried to reason with her. But under alcohol's influence, reason was not something that easily leaped off the tongue. Logic told me that whatever we had experienced was not because of some pissed off Creator God getting His vengeance. It was just bad people, doing bad things. And we just had to deal with it.

But as we got closer to the drop-off point, I couldn't help but feel some nefarious evil was at work. I knew I couldn't face it, whatever it was, alone. I would have to depend on Compton and the others to get through what was coming our way.

I glanced at Compton, whose eyes were drilled forward, his rifle in hand, ready to dispatch anyone that got in the way of our mission.

"There they are," Compton called out.

CHAPTER 33

Ron

There were two vehicles waiting for us at the agreed upon meet-up place.

"The big tree, in between the two blockades," as Trunk had explained, "is where you'll meet. You'll find a large swath of snow that we plowed aside to allow our vehicles or his to turn around before they went too far."

We approached a colossal leafless oak, mostly caked in snow and ice, under which two of McBoyd's idling vehicles were facing us.

I softly pedaled the brakes until we stopped, giving us some distance in case everything went to shit.

"Follow my lead, Ronald," Compton demanded.

I nodded. "Yes."

"Honey, you can lead me anywhere, anytime," Patsy said from behind us, placing her hand on his shoulder. Her other hand was on Millie, who had stretched from the jumper seat so that her head was on Patsy's shoulder the entire trip.

"Patsy, quit flirting with our captors," barked Wilma, sitting beside her. Patsy kept a hand on Compton and eyed her mother in a show of protest.

My sense was that I was the only one who was nervous about what would happen next. A big part of me wished that Joey was behind this wheel instead of me. Joey knew how to handle himself, and he and Compton thought alike in these kinds of situations. But before leaving, we agreed that Bobby McBoyd was too unpredictable and might hurt Joey if he were here.

The wind had abated, and I could better see that Bobby was in the driver's seat of the bigger of the two trucks. The smaller one, parked behind Bobby, had several men inside. My AR pistol was already in my lap, checked and rechecked. I wiped the sweaty palm of my pistol grip hand once more on my pant leg and waited for that moment.

"Okay, here's how this is going to go," Compton said, addressing all of us. "Everyone but Ronald here is going to get out of the truck slowly, so that McBoyd can see who's here. Then when I tell you, you'll start moving forward past me. I'll follow behind to make sure they don't try something funny. Do you understand?"

He looked at each of us for acknowledgment. "And Ronald," he said, glaring only at me now, "you'll have your door open, and your weapon steadied on the frame, aimed at anyone who is a potential threat. If one of them appears to be ready to fire their weapon, you fire first. Got it?"

"Got it," I responded and swallowed, even though my mouth was desert dry.

Everyone was already zipped or buttoned up, so when Compton said, "Let's go," all doors opened at the same time, and they stepped out. I clicked open my driver's side door, moved a foot to the outside runner and rose from my seat. My gun barrel came to rest on the area where the open door met the frame. I had to move more outside to sight through my right eye, while watching what happened next through my left.

My heart beat like a bongo drum, but I think I was pretty calm. Still, I did what I found myself doing more often than not lately. I said a quick prayer that we would somehow get out of this safely.

Compton stepped forward, past the truck's bumper. He turned toward the others and said "...forward," but I couldn't hear him very well.

Bobby McBoyd's truck door popped open, and he stepped out and glared in our direction. "Wait, Millie," cried Patsy.

Millie shot forward from our truck and zoomed right at him, like a big brown bullet of fur. Bobby looked startled, ready to flee. Then he mouthed words at the Shepherd, who stopped right beside him and sat obediently. Bobby, still speaking, wagged a finger at the dog, who shrank to the ground.

You can sure tell a lot about a person by how their dog reacts to them. Millie definitely did not care for her master, and neither did I.

The truck behind Bobby then emptied. Each of the men stepped out, eyeballed us and positioned their rifles at the ready. I fixed my sights on each man for a quick moment before moving on to the next. My finger twitched above the trigger guard, ready to engage in a millisecond.

Then two things happened which were a complete shock to me, and I venture to everyone else.

George and Smittie walked around and in front of our truck, as did Wilma McBoyd from the passenger side. They marched toward McBoyd's truck. But Patsy McBoyd held back, stopping in front of Compton. She tugged on

Compton's arm to get his attention. Upon doing so, she leaned toward him and kissed him softly on the lips. She stood for a moment smiling, looking like she was going to join the others, but that's when the first unexpected thing happened.

Compton grabbed both of Patsy's arms and kissed her back. It was a long and passionate kiss, which lasted for several slow seconds. Then he released her.

Not a word was said between them. She turned her back to him and rather than walking away, she skipped, like a little girl finally released from a long day of school. She caught up and passed the others, as she headed toward the first truck and Bobby McBoyd's outstretched arms.

Bobby mouthed words to the returning captives, who were already standing before him. In my position, it was impossible to hear anything. Smittie nodded and opened the rear passenger door of Bobby's truck and ducked inside. George followed and then closed the door. Bobby said something to Millie, who ran around the back of the truck and jumped into the truck bed. Bobby entered his truck, closed his door, and then glared his impatience at the women.

Wilma hung for a moment before opening the front passenger door and beckoning her daughter to follow. Patsy was gazing in our direction—no, at Compton. A smile hung on her face, and she waved at Compton furiously before turning back to follow Wilma into the front of the truck.

Compton startled me, swiftly entering our vehicle, and immediately slamming the door. "Quit your grinning, Ash," he demanded.

I couldn't help it. It was damned cute.

With my door still open, I returned my sights to the men from the truck behind Bobby. They still hadn't returned to their truck.

That's when the second unexpected thing happened.

Each of the men still had their hands on their weapons, slung in front of them. But they stood in their positions and looked confused about their next move. Each kept their eyes on Bobby's truck, as if waiting to hear their next order. I thought, Oh no, here it comes now. Then all of them looked down... at their feet.

I glanced over at Compton. He too was looking down at the floorboards. Instantly, I understood why.

"Is it me," he said. "Or is the earth moving?"

CHAPTER 34

Ron

The earth is moving.

My brain tried to reason that it was only our vehicle rough idling. But that wouldn't explain why the men behind Bobby's truck appeared to be steadying themselves, without much luck. The ground was heaving below them as well.

"Earthquake," I announced.

A moment later, either the shaking underneath our Landcruiser had increased, altering our perspective, or the giant oak tree had been jolted violently. It rocked to one side, away from Bobby's truck. The men still standing in between him and the second truck, as well as those now on the ground, all looked up at the menacing tree above them. Then the tree swayed in the other direction, toward the trucks.

I could hear the yelling now.

Compton must have sensed what was about to happen next as he dashed out of his seat, leaving his door open. I left a second later.

The tree jerked forward, and with it, an ear-wrenching crack sounded.

Most of Bobby's men were attempting to flee the inevitable, like rats on a sinking ship. Compton and I tried to get there, but the ground below our feet kept lurching. We were halfway there when the tree collapsed, crashing down on top of Bobby's truck, crushing much of it, and probably most everyone in it.

Nan

Dog began to bark, I thought because he missed his new friend Millie. But Leticia knew immediately that it was something more menacing.

"We need to get to the strongest part of the house," Leticia stated as if reading from one of her books.

"Why, honey?" Suzie asked.

Dog howled and all of us were now on our feet, not sure what Dog and Leticia sensed that we somehow could not.

"Because an earthquake is about to h—"

She couldn't finish her sentence before we were sent to our knees, and the whole house shook like a broken theme park ride.

God, I hate these things, I thought.

"The fireplace," Suzie yelled and attempted to get up and move toward the stone fireplace that dominated their living room. But before she could even take a step, she was sent backwards, onto the floor.

I vividly remembered that these things leveled my concrete apartment building, sending blocks down on top of Ron, and nearly killing him. A fireplace couldn't be much better. I eyed the dining room. "No, the dining room table." I grabbed Leticia's arm and we duck-walked there.

Dog joined us underneath. Then Suzie.

"Cover your head and neck," Leticia instructed and then demonstrated.

Other than Dog, who woofed at the unseen earthquake, we each followed Leticia's lead. We waited for it to stop, hoping we wouldn't get crushed before it did.

I wondered where Ron and the others were.

Suzie sang out The Lord's Prayer in a shaky voice. I think I joined in.

Ron

Then the earthquake stopped.

Our feet found terra firma and we were at Bobby's crushed truck in a shot.

The tree had fallen across the driver's side of the truck, striking the driver's door first, then stretching across the length of the pickup, telegraphing past its now flattened bed. There was no way to get to the survivors from the driver's side. So we attacked the passenger side. Compton attempted to tug on the passenger front door, and I reached for the rear door. Mine opened easily, while Compton grunted and swore at his.

George Halston looked down at me in a daze; the left side of his head had a gash and a healthy flow of red seeped from it. Across from him, on the other side of the seat, should have been an open space and then another person. It was gone.

There, the truck's roof had collapsed. Having been vise-gripped down by the multi-ton tree, it left barely an inch between it and the seat. That compressed area looked as if it had just come out of a car compacting machine, like in a junkyard. Unsuccessfully co-occupying that space was McBoyd's freckle-faced nephew, Smittie. Or what was left of him. Only an outstretched arm remained unmolested. It flopped over onto George's seat when George moved toward me.

No one could have survived that.

George lifted himself from his seat and I pulled him outside, while Compton came around the door, hollering, "I can't get to Patsy and Wilma. The door won't open."

"Here," I said, reaching down to one of the seat's side levers. Pulling up, the front passenger seat back disengaged. It fell back, revealing a disoriented Patsy McBride, who blinked her eyes in an attempt to gain clarity.

"Compton, you get her," I said. "I'll get Wilma." I hopped up into the back seat, avoiding Smittie's seemingly severed arm, and gazed at Wilma, sitting in the middle seat, moaning. Surprisingly, Bobby's area of the cab was not crushed as bad as Smittie's. But it was still bad. And Bobby was either unconscious or dead because he wasn't moving.

Compton reached in beside me to pull out Patsy by her arms. He made it quick and when her passenger seat was unoccupied, I crawled into it. I needed better leverage to get to Wilma. "I'm going to need help with Wilma and Bobby," I yelled.

Wilma turned her head to me and said in a weak voice, "Please help Bobby first."

"We have to get you out, Wilma. Then we can get to Bobby," I told her. Then I put my hands under her arms and hoisted her onto the horizontal seat back so that Compton could get her the rest of the way out from the rear.

When I attempted to pull on Bobby, I could feel his left side was like a pulpy mess. His head flopped forward, and I almost thought it might fall right off his body. I hesitated, afraid of what damage I might do by pulling any more.

"He's dead if we leave him there," said Compton, kneeling on the rear seat, leaning toward me. "He might have a chance if we can get him out and get him to Suzie Halston."

I gritted my teeth and tugged Bobby sideways. He came loose. "I think his left side is crushed," I instructed while maneuvering him closer to Compton. I could see his leg was bleeding badly too.

"Got 'im," he said, heaving on Bobby's right arm and shoulder, until finally, Bobby was in the back seat.

In two quick moves, Compton had Bobby out of the truck and then on his back, doing the fireman's carry. "Come on. Everyone back to our vehicle."

"Halt," yelled a voice from behind the truck. As I crawled out, I saw it was one of McBoyd's men, pointing his rifle at us. "Put them in our truck," commanded the rifleman.

Compton didn't abate, jogging as fast as he could under McBoyd's considerable weight for our Landcruiser. Upon reflection, I should have attempted to move the truck closer.

"Whoa," I said, standing in front of the man, who attempted to keep his weapon trained on Compton. "Do you have a doctor or nurse at McBoyd's? Well, Suzie Halston is a doctor." I was pretty sure she was only a nurse, but for our purposes, she was a doctor.

The man looked befuddled, lowering his weapon.

Then I saw George. Surprisingly, he emerged from the back of the truck, cradling Millie in his arms. In all the craziness, I had forgotten about the McBoyds' Shepherd. Before he passed me, he mumbled something like, "Wouldn't be right to leave a dog to die." He waddled toward the Landcruiser.

"Thanks, George," Patsy said.

"Come on," I said, putting an arm around Wilma and Patsy, leading them away. "We can all go to the Halstons'." I followed George's path, who followed Compton, quick walking the two women to our vehicle. All the while, I wondered if I was going to be shot by one of McBoyd's men.

"Get in front, Patsy," Compton directed. She was the least hurt of any of them. "George in the jump seat in back." Compton put Bobby in the back seat with him and Wilma. He must of had some battlefield medicine training, because he used his belt to tourniquet Bobby's leg.

As I climbed in, the Landcruiser came alive with voices.

"Is he dead?" Wilma screeched.

"Oh my God, Daddy, can you hear me?" Patsy cried.

"Quiet," Compton barked. "Ronald, get us to Halston's on the double."

I had already spun us around in a U-turn, and upon Compton's words, I stomped on the gas. McBoyd's smaller truck was filled again with all of his armed men. They raced to keep up with us.

Just before we arrived at Halston's drive, Compton began CPR on Bobby McBoyd and Wilma passed out. But there was another problem ahead of us.

The Halstons' unmanned gate was bent at an odd angle, as was some of the fencing. Worse, above the trees encircling Halston's home, black smoke rose in the air. No one was going to open up for us.

"Hold on," I said before I gassed the engine and plowed through the Halstons' gate.

CHAPTER 35

Nan

When the shaking stopped, the silence was fleeting. Almost immediately, the house sounded like it was collapsing in on itself.

"What is that?" I yelled through a building noise of mortar and stone crumbling.

A muffled voice outside cried, "Watch... chimney!"

We glared at the walk-in fireplace. It still appeared to be shaking.

At a grinding crescendo, stones rained down the chimney's firebox, some tumbling out, over the hearth and across the hardwood.

A muffled boom sounded, and a cloud of dusty ash came billowing into the living room, momentarily veiling the room in gray.

We covered our mouths, closed our eyes, and stood up from the dining room table, waiting for it to pass.

When the soot-laden fog finally settled, we could see the damage.

A wing-back armchair had been shot backwards, broken from heavy chimney stones. Its mate was sent sideways. The fireplace they had sat in front of was an unrecognizable pile of stone and debris.

"Thank you," Suzie said, her voice hoarse and wobbly. She scooped away a tranche of hair from her eyes, and a layer of grit fell from her.

"What for?" I asked and then coughed.

"For not listening to me. We would have been crushed if we had sought cover by the fireplace."

"Thank Leticia. She's the one who had the coolest head of all of us," I said, shining a smile at Leticia. She tilted her head down, lightly coated in gray. She feigned embarrassment, and let a grin break loose.

Suzie aggressively pulled her hair back over her shoulders and then slapped loose some more of the ash that still clung to her arms. She looked around the room and said, "Would you two check to make sure no one was hurt inside the house?" She began quick stepping toward the front door. "I'm going to check the outside."

Leticia and I split up, Dog following Leticia. I headed toward the bedrooms and she toward the kitchen.

The first bedroom appeared empty but for Bigelow, who was hiding under his covers. I could see his shivering mound underneath. "It's over, Bigelow. You can come out now," I hollered into the bedroom, before shutting the door and moving to the other rooms.

Working my way to the last bedroom where Chloe was sleeping, I could see the damage was limited to just breakage of little things and a few cracks in the plasterboard. So far, nothing serious and thankfully no one injured. The Halstons' home was obviously well constructed because it had withstood more than one earthquake since this whole thing started.

"I need help," Suzie bellowed from the front.

I ran to find Suzie coming in from the outside. With one arm, she supported one of the Halstons' workers. Lou-Something. He was bloodied from head to toe. His leg looked seriously damaged.

I offered to support the man's other side, as Leticia came running into the living room. "Can I help?" Chloe asked, followed by Dog. Other than Chloe's short hair being mussed, she looked uninjured too.

"Let's go to the first bedroom," Suzie said. "That will be our infirmary if we need it. Leticia, can you get my doctor's bag? It's by Chloe's bed."

Lou was out of it, but we got him inside the bedroom. Bigelow finally arose from his covers to find out what was causing all of the commotion. He glanced at me, and I gave him a don't-say-anything look, and he didn't utter a word. He knew better.

Suzie laid Lou down on a bed and got to work inspecting his wounds. "Nan, Lou should be fine. Could you go back outside and see if anyone else is hurt? Maybe check in the fields?"

"Absolutely," I acknowledged, and turned to head out as Leticia arrived with the black leather case. Suzie hollered some instructions to Chloe and Leticia as I left. But all I could hear was Dog barking again.

Ron

It was not as bad as I had feared.

The Halstons' log-pole home looked intact, but for one side. I wasn't sure what I was looking at, until we pulled up to the front door.

On the living room side of the home, where only an hour ago, a towering chimney stood, there was now an accumulation of stones, piled up against the house like a crude buttress to keep the rest of the home from falling over. A huge oak tree, not unlike the one that had crushed McBoyd's truck, was lying roots-up on top of the pile.

Although not good, if that was the extent of the major damage, then the Halstons got away much better than I would have guessed.

More concerning was the smoke coming from the growing buildings, or what the Halstons called the Fields. And farther in the distance, a separate plume of black smoke gathered in the sky, perhaps from the McBoyds'.

Two of Halston's people were dashing from the house to the Fields.

When we parked, I saw blood across the home's front door threshold. I ignored this, focusing instead on what we had to do. I honked the truck's horn and swung out of my seat.

"George, get the front door," commanded Compton, who was already out of the truck and once again hoisting an unconscious Bobby McBoyd on his back.

"I've got Wilma," I told Patsy, who although she appeared in a daze, was trying to help me with her mom. Wilma was now alert and moaning. I could see the source of her pain, as her left side looked bloodied. Until Suzie had a look at it, I didn't want it touched.

George was at the door, tiptoeing around the blood. He was about to open it, when the door flew inward, revealing Nan and Dog.

I held up when I saw them.

Nan stepped out, over the threshold, blinking her eyes and coughing. Dog sneezed repeatedly. Both were covered in a fine layer of gray soot.

Nan

"Are you all right?" Ron asked with a grunt, while supporting most of Wilma's weight as she stepped out of the truck.

"You?" I asked, moving aside when he shook his head at my offer of support. I could see why: Her left arm was bloodied, misshapen and looked broken. From the other side of the truck, Compton carried an older man on his back. This one looked much worse off. "Go to the first bedroom," I instructed. "That's our infirmary. Suzie is there."

Patsy nodded and followed them through the front door. I caught a glimpse of George standing off to the side. I was about to say, "What the hell was he doing here?" But then I saw he was cradling McBoyd's dog, Millie.

"Come on, you better bring her inside too."

CHAPTER 36

Leticia

Mrs. Halston was amazing. She must have run an emergency room because she was giving out commands to everyone, including her husband, and we were all following. But what was most amazing to me was that they were breaking their backs trying to save their so-called enemies... As well as Dog's new friend Millie, who was also hurt, but not bad.

Millie had a broken leg, but Mrs. Halston was worried about internal injuries too. Even though she was a Christian woman, she cursed about not having a fluoroscope.

Dog was there, by Millie's bed. He stuck his nose beside Millie's and moaned slightly. Millie whimpered back. It was very sweet. After a little while, Dog turned in place a couple of times and then lay down in a heap, giving a moan as he put his head down. He wasn't going anywhere, staying to protect and make sure his princess was better.

Mrs. McBoyd was in worse shape, though not horribly. Evidently the tree that fell on them crushed several of her bones. And because Mrs. Halston could only do remedial surgery, she said Wilma would survive with life-long pain and never regain full use of her left arm. Again, Mrs.

Halston was worried about internal injuries that she couldn't see. And if she had them, she probably would not make it through the day.

Mr. McBoyd was the worst. When he came to, he protested initially. Then Mrs. Halston calmed him down and told him that his wife and daughter were absolutely fine. I understood that she was telling him a white lie, for his own benefit. Then she told him the bad news: His leg was crushed, and it would have to be amputated, or he would probably die.

He said many bad words, which I won't repeat, including some I'd never heard of before. I made a mental note of them to ask Nan later what each of them meant. She seemed to have a larger bad-word vocabulary than Ronald.

When Mr. McBoyd calmed down again, he told her that there was no way he was allowing some bad-word, fake doctor cut on him.

Mrs. Halston, nodded, never getting emotional about what he called her. I would have been angry at the things he said. Instead, she was gracious and told him that she would do what she could for him. He then told her that he felt like he would fall asleep too soon; he insisted that she give him a shot of adrenalin so that he would stay awake to make sure nothing happened to his wife. She agreed to this too.

You might call it opportunistic, but I knew then I would have to interview him at that moment. He was alert now, and it sounded like he might not make it through the night. I felt pretty guilty even thinking it. But then I darted from the room and ran back to the women's bedroom to grab my recorder and a new SD card.

Upon my return, a soft argument drew my attention to the living room. I was too nosy not to check it out. At the edge of the hallway, their conversation was loud and clear.

"You really should stay here with your mother and father."

I peeked around the corner and confirmed it was Compton speaking to Patsy McBoyd.

"You were only going because I said I was going," Patsy argued. "No, I'm going and you're staying."

"What do you mean, no—" Before he could finish, Patsy kissed him on his lips.

She withdrew and asked, "Is this our first argument?"

He was about to say something, and she kissed him again.

Until Compton became my friend, I thought he was mean and scary looking. But I learned that for all his rough edges, deep down, he was a kind and considerate person. Now, seeing the two of them, I couldn't help but feel happy.

"Here's the deal," Patsy said, her voice low and serious. "I'm either going alone or with you. My cousins are not going to let you go there on your own. After all, you're the one who abducted me. So I accept your offer to accompany me home. And I know Suzie will do what she can for my parents. But I may be able to help others."

She grabbed his hand. "Come on, let's go see what happened to the rest of my family, and my home." They breezed out the door, together.

I turned back to the bedroom to get my interview with Mr. McBoyd.

The whole time, I wondered where Ronald was.

CHAPTER 37

Ron

After dropping off the McBoyds into Suzie's capable hands, I turned my attention to the fire I had seen by The Fields.

From the house, it appeared that the smoke had dissipated some. But as I approached, thick puffs of black were still seeping out of the nearest and farthest buildings. It was one or more fires and they appeared out of control. I ran for the closest building, which contained all the machinery.

As soon as I opened the door, dense smoke poured out, and so did steam. Lots and lots of steam.

"Is anyone here?" I yelled into the heated cloud, and then stepped back because it was too hot near the doorway. The plumes billowed out, turning whiter as they met with the cold air outside.

When I first saw the smoke, I had suspected that that some piece of machinery had been sent out of whack from the earthquake. But the large quantity of steam indicated another, perhaps larger, problem. Trunk had channeled the steam coming from the geothermal vents to the engine which generated their electricity, and the excess steam was sent directly to the growing buildings and his home to create radiant heat. It shouldn't be pouring into this building unless a line broke or something else was happening.

At least the machinery was off, so they weren't causing any further damage. But the steam was not dissipating, and the room was still too hot to approach, much less walk through. So I decided to hoof it to the outside entrance at the end of the farthest building.

This is a poor design, I thought as I worked my way as quickly as I could over the trampled path of snow running parallel to the long line of buildings. Trunk said he saved on the steel buildings by having each of them connect one after the other. It was also a horrible safety hazard. If you're trapped in one of the middle buildings, there's no way to get out, unless you happened to be carrying an oxy-acetylene torch on you.

When I made it to the final building, I was gasping for air and had to stop to recover. I hadn't even considered what to do if the oversized door was locked. Other than when they first brought animals inside, I gathered this door was only used as an exit.

I hesitated before touching the handle, as the whole door was perspiring from it being heated on the other side. And smoke still appeared to be coming out of the vents at the top.

A quick touch of the door told me the fire wasn't on the other side. I reached to turn the handle, but before I could, the door flew inward. Out poured smoke and a cacophony of sounds poured out from the doorway: bleating sheep, frantic birds, wailing moos, and scared people.

At the door, a man led a blindfolded horse outside, followed by another.

I quickly tied the bandanna that I kept in my pocket over my mouth and darted in when no one was coming through.

Trunk was leading two goats on ropes up the ramp to the door. He looked up and saw me. "Ron. Glad you're here. Please grab some of the kids from the paddock."

Admittedly, I thought he really meant human children, when I realized he was talking about the baby goats. "Sure," I said and dashed down the side stairs to the goat enclosure, on the other side of the building.

Once there, I saw the problem. Thick smoke was sliding through the gap under the door, leading to the next building.

The corn. It's on fire.

When I opened the gate to the corral, the dozen or so little goats rushed out and headed for the open doorway at the other end. My mind fixated on the larger issue: how to put out the fire in the next building.

Surely, they had a watering system. But where?

I swung my AR pistol around and clicked on its light. It was fastened to the lower receiver's picatinny rail and shot out a beam directly in front of me.

"Where are you?" I asked my light to show me, illuminating the bottom of the wall that met the ground. A gaggle of angry geese attempted to peck at me when I found the incoming water line. It came through the back side of the building, right next to the steam vent, which was connected to an over-sized radiator. I was perspiring profusely at this point, not only from the exercise, but from the heat being emitted from the thing. It hit me then.

Behind the radiator was the vent, which ran through a one-foot round opening in the steel.

"That would work," I said out loud.

"What are you searching for, Ron?" Trunk asked from behind me.

"A way to put out the fire in the corn field, next door," I said.

"If we open the door to get a hose in, we'll—"

"Not that," I interrupted; we didn't have time. "Although you might want to get some water on that door and wall."

"Good idea," Trunk said, turning away from me. "Don, get water on the door..."

While Trunk was directing one of his men, I was looking for something I could use. I trotted over to several tools, up against a nearby wall, and grabbed exactly what I needed.

"What..." Trunk tried to ask me, but I was already running for the exit.

"Follow me with help and a tool belt," I hollered behind me.

Outside the door the animals looked calm, as if nothing had happened earlier. I glanced around for Trunk. He was behind me, telling another to follow.

I headed for the back side of the building, hoisting the heavy digging bar over a shoulder and trudging through the heavy snow.

Near the other end of the building, where it connected to the building where the fire was blazing, my path got easier. The big conduit which vented the steam into each building's radiators, although heavily insulated, still emitted a fair amount of heat, melting a parallel path through the snow and ice several inches beside it.

"What in God's name do you have in mind, Ron?" Trunk asked, catching up to me.

"We're going to vent the steam into the corn building," I said, stopping in front of the first radiator vent. "I'm going to need you to pull the conduit away from the vent first, and I'm afraid that's going to be difficult because the steam is hotter than normal."

Either Trunk and I were on the same page, or he fully trusted me, as he grabbed an adjustable ratchet and started to work on the clamps holding the flex ducting to the vents, while instructing a teenager who accompanied him to pull and keep the vent in front of him.

They did as requested and when it was free, I drove the heavy flat end of the wrecking bar into the vent and the radiator on the other side. With a deep thud, it came loose and felt like it flopped over. Black smoke immediately emptied out of the vent hole.

"Okay, now replace it," I had to yell, "while I get to work on the next one." I grabbed the ratchet and the trusty bar and scurried to the second radiator vent.

In a few short minutes, we had channeled billowing clouds of super-heated steam into the burning corn fields. Although it was hot, the water would condense on the sides of the building, from the outside cold and eventually smother the fire.

Later, Nan, Leticia and a reluctant Bigelow came to help. By the end of the day, the fire was out, and we had determined the source of the fire. The earthquake knocked a bank of grow lights down from the ceiling, still connected to the building's electricity, sparking the fire. The corn was lost, but Trunk had more seeds stored away for just such an emergency.

The power plant was a larger issue. It would take a few days to repair all the damage caused by the earthquake and increased pressure to the line. However, before the end of day, we were able to channel the excess steam coming from the geothermal vent to the outside. This relieved the excess pressure which had caused a break in the incoming steam line that I witnessed in the first building.

This increase in pressure—I'm guessing it had to be at least a ten-fold increase—must have also been due to the earthquake.

What was not mentioned the entire day was the fact that the earthquake and Bobby McBoyd's injuries averted the inevitable attack at noon and subsequent loss of life.

CHAPTER 38

Compton

Patsy had no trouble convincing the men who had followed us from the drop-off—one of them a cousin—to return with us to the McBoyd residence and check on everyone's status. As she told them, "We are going, whether you follow us or not."

Patsy was adamant about checking on the rest of her family. The Halston place, which was definitely well constructed, out of some fine materials, had weathered the earthquake with minimal damage. So the hope was that the McBoyds weren't any worse off.

Getting there was my initial worry.

Admittedly, our ingress to McBoyd's was complicated by my diversion. I had planted my tannerite charge in a tree well, intending that it make a lot of noise and perhaps knock down a tree onto the road to slow down any pursuit. It was not intended to hurt, and certainly not intended to take out a vehicle, much less one with Leticia in it. That guilt will always be on me the rest of my days.

With Ronald's shovel attachment, we were able to push aside the damaged vehicle and two fallen trees, and we drove right up to McBoyd's home.

"Oh my God, C," Patsy moaned as she caught a glimpse of the severe damage to the main structure.

She shrieked and jumped out of the Landcruiser before I could bring us to a stop. The partially opened door frame was twisted and listing at an awkward angle, but it didn't slow her down. With the agility of a gymnast, she slipped through.

"Be careful!" I hollered as I hopped out, grabbing the crowbar Ronald kept under the seat. "That thing could come down any mo—" But she was already out of sight.

My shoulders were substantially larger than Patsy's and weren't meant to make it through the small opening: I had considered going to a different entrance, when I heard Patsy scream. Ignoring my concerns that if I pushed too hard the whole thing would topple down, I stepped through and away from the doorway. It shook a little but remained.

Patsy was standing over a body, weeping.

"We-we practically grew up together," she struggled to say.

I put a finger on the man's carotid and confirmed what she already knew. A heavy table lay on top of his pelvis, probably crushing him.

A small piece of drywall fell from the ceiling and hit nearby, causing both of us to jump.

"Patsy, it's not safe here," I said. "Let's quickly check for others."

She nodded, wiped her face and stood. She turned to me and whispered, "Thanks for coming with me. I couldn't do this alone."

She maneuvered around a fallen chandelier and stepped carefully through other debris, toward a hallway. "Is anyone here?" she called out.

I gave a brief glance around the room in case she didn't check and maybe missed anyone else. Shafts of light poured through broken areas in the masonry walls and from an opening in roof. But there was no one.

"In here," Patsy called, her voice shaky.

She was standing in the doorway of what looked like an office, with her head tilted away. "Could you check him too, C? I just can't do it." Inside, a man with a rifle lay unmoving under a fallen bookcase.

I didn't need to check this man's vitals. The metal bookcase had glass shelves, one of which was broken and sticking out of the man's back.

"Come on," I insisted, grabbing her hand. "Let's check the rest of the house together."

We did, and thankfully we found no other casualties. The front part of the house, the original structure, was not structurally sound. However, the back part of the house was completely stable and almost undamaged. It was stick-built and added when building laws required more rigorous construction than the 1800s when the first part of the structure was built.

After dealing with the dead, we sealed off the broken front structure from the back. Then we settled in for the night in Patsy's room, were we first met.

Late that evening, Patsy turned to me and asked, "You're not planning on fighting in Father's stupid war, are you?"

There was no light in the room, so I couldn't see her expression. But with her body pressed to mine, and her head against my arm, I could feel her start to shudder. A tear splashed on my chest.

"I was about to leave for Mexico, as I figured it had to be warmer, when your father delivered his ultimatum. And..." I wanted to say, 'And you came along, changing everything...' Only I didn't.

We lay under the covers of her bed, keeping each other warm, until we finally fell asleep.

A thundering, whooshing sound woke me in the morning. I sat up, pistol in hand, ready to take on whomever or whatever was a threat. But only Patsy was there beside me.

"Damn! I swear the earth is against us," Patsy said with a chuckle. She was already sitting up, wrapped in a giant patchwork blanket. "You are the quietest sleeper I've ever slept beside."

"What..." I started to ask, not sure I heard her correctly over the constant hiss outside.

"You thought you were my first?" she asked, her playful smile fully fixed to her face.

"No, I was trying to ask what is that noise?"

"I have my suspicions. But I haven't heard it in years."

"Get dressed," I said as I buckled my pants. "Then you can tell me what you think that is."

She watched me dress, as I did her, though I tried to keep my mind on the mission at hand.

We stepped outside and then walked to the end of a full-length balcony that wrapped around her second-story bedroom.

In the back corner of the property were several steel buildings, similar to those on Trunk's property. In front of the middle building was a recessed well, out of which erupted a large plume of steam and water. The plume billowed upward into the sky.

Patsy put her arms around me and yelled over the noisy vent, "Will you take me with you... You know, to Mexico?"

"That may not be necessary," I said and smiled at her.

I asked first about what she remembered and then I told her why I said what I did.

At this she bounded from her grasp of me and dashed into her bedroom. She emerged with my backpack.

"Are you all right?" I asked.

"Yes, of course. I'm better than all right. I just want to tell Daddy the news: That there is no reason to fight the Halstons anymore."

CHAPTER 39

Nan

When the Landcruiser screeched to a halt on the other side of the front door, I went outside to find out what new calamity had hit us, or was about to hit us.

Patsy was first out of her seat, followed quickly by Compton, who looked different. Almost happy. I'm not sure I had ever seen him really smile.

Patsy waited for him, grabbed his hand and they both ran toward the door. It was as clear as a Dick and Jane book. They were a couple, but it was Patsy who was positively bursting with happiness.

And I was the one who was about to destroy her joy.

"Wait!" I said, blocking their entry into the house.

"Nan, we need to tell McBoyd and Halston something important," Compton huffed.

There was no good way to say what I had to say, so I just spit it out. "Patsy, your father is dead. His injuries were too—"

"No!" Patsy screamed. "Mama?" she begged, releasing Compton's hand, and slowing in front of me.

"She'll make it. She..."

Patsy didn't wait to hear the details. She dashed past me through the door.

Compton walked by. "Come on, Nan. You can tell us both. And then we can tell you our news." He marched toward Suzie's makeshift infirmary and disappeared inside.

I found Patsy there, hugging her mom, both of them sobbing. The bed next to them contained Bobby's lifeless form, a sheet pulled over his rotund body. Suzie stood nearby, looking at the McBoyds solemnly.

Compton and Ron were having an animated conversation on the other side of the room. Chloe and Joey were sitting in the next bed, listening.

Trunk entered, his gaze finding first me and then the McBoyd women. He flashed a weak grin to his wife and headed toward her.

Wilma then pushed her daughter away and asked, "Besides Danny and Timothy, where there any others injured?"

"No," Patsy said, wiping her eyes. "But there was a lot of damage to the house. And..."

Compton and Ron marched over to Suzie and Trunk.

Patsy looked up to Compton. "C, could you explain what we found?"

"Sure," Compton said. "Of course, Bobby's death already changes everything. But there is something good that has come out of this earthquake."

I had ambled closer. So had Chloe and Joey. Even Bigelow, who I hadn't realized was sleeping in his bed in the corner, had gotten out of bed to hear what Compton was about to say.

"I've just confirmed it with Ronald. Not only do the McBoyds have their hot springs back, both you"—Compton said this to Patsy and Wilma—"and the

Halstons have more than enough geothermal venting to power and heat a city."

Ron added, "Either the earthquake has opened up a new geothermal vent or it dislodged something, opening up an old one, perhaps making it bigger. Because the Halstons have over ten times the pressure coming from their vent now."

Trunk took a step forward, "And Wilma, I know I speak for my wife, and I believe our family... We will do everything in our power to help you get to a place where you can generate heat and power like we are here. And I will share my seeds and animal stock so you too can be self-sustaining. But..."

Trunk turned to us, his glare hanging on Ron. "But there's no way we can do it without your help, Ron. And all of your friends' help."

Wilma had swung her feet out of her bed and was walking toward us, Patsy just behind her.

Her red eyes welled up some more and her lower lip quivered. She attempted to smile at Trunk and then Suzie. Tears started to stream down her cheeks."I'm so sorry for what Bobby has done to you. And I am more sorry that I didn't stand up to him and make him stop. The war died with Bobby and as far as I'm concerned it is over between our two families."

She slung her uninjured arm around Trunk and kissed him on his cheek. Suzie grabbed Wilma's hand and gently squeezed it. In response, I saw Trunk mouth the words, "As I have been forgiven, I forgive you."

"Thank you," Wilma said, before she let a fit of sobs take control of her, while loosely hugging Trunk and Suzie.

She let go and then faced us. "I have no right to ask any of you anything. My family treated you so poorly when we should have invited you in..." Her eyes leaked some more. "You certainly don't have any obligation to help us. But I'm pleading with you to please stay and help us do what Trunk said he would try to do?"

All of us were quiet for a while, letting it all set into our minds: They were asking us to stay there for a long enough period to help the McBoyds get back on their feet, and make sure the Halstons were in good shape, before we even considered leaving, first to Colorado and then finally to our destination, Wyoming.

Probably because no one said anything, Trunk asked, "Well, would you folks stay for a few weeks more, to help us and the McBoyds? And of course, as I offered before, you're welcome to stay forever."

Ron looked at me and I nodded. Then he looked at Joey and Chloe and they nodded. Then, surprisingly, Compton nodded at Ron too. Leticia, who was sitting next to Dog and Millie, stood. "Dog and I agree."

"What?" hollered Bigelow. "There is no fu—"

Compton slapped Bigelow on the cheek, cutting him off mid-expletive. Bigelow snapped his mouth shut, scowled for a moment and then let his head droop forward as he nodded. "That makes all of us," Compton stated and then smiled.

Two Months Later

CHAPTER 40

Nan

The Halstons' living room, like our world, had been transformed.

Even though I'd been involved in every step of its transformation, I still had to blink several times to make sure I was seeing it correctly. The picture window across the room provided the perfect juxtaposition between the outside world and the one we all crafted inside. It was the difference between where we could have been if we had not come together and where we were today.

Outside was frozen and deadly.

Inside was alive with the warmth of friends and members from two previously warring families, all sitting together in their seats, waiting expectantly for the wedding to begin.

Outside were two shades of white, formed by a blanket of snow and ice, framed by unrelentingly ominous clouds.

Inside was a cornucopia of warm tones and vibrant colors: the reds and oranges of the crackling fire; multi-colored strings of faux flowers created by Chloe and Leticia, which ran around the room, as well as were individually woven around each of the number of seats broken into two sections; the bounty of hues from the dried plants Suzie crafted from what they'd grown and then Leticia worked around the books in the library area and around the fireplace; the imitation rose petals scattered along the aisle, which bisected the seats, all leading up to a long-stemmed candle holder with two unlit candles...

There was a rap on the window and a wave from Ron. He gave a thumbs-up and then promptly disappeared.

He made it! Barely.

Although he said he had one last modification to make in the growing buildings and he'd be done before the ceremony started, I wasn't too sure he would get here on time. He should have put it off for one more day. We would have waited. But he insisted, no doubt for our benefit, and in the process, he was almost late for this big day.

I looked back over to the focus of the room. Trunk, looking nice dressed in a suit, was front and center of the room, holding a Bible. His face was the definition of happiness.

Joey was standing to his left, fidgeting in an oversized tuxedo that Trunk had lent him. Beside Joey was Compton, who was his usual stoic self, but also dressed in a fancy suit that Wilma had given him. Most surprising was that both men had shaved off their beards and mustaches. I had not seen either without facial hair.

The music started.

In the opposite corner of the living room/wedding venue, Suzie began playing the Wedding March. She smiled widely from behind her baby grand piano. It had been moved diagonally across to the other side of the living room to make room for all the guests to sit and witness this event.

Everyone rose from their seats. Ron, who must have quietly slipped in from the dining room, squeezed my arm to let me know he was in fact here, just in time. I smiled at him and then he disappeared down the hallway, as I realized that he had magically changed into nicer clothes. Though the pants were a couple of sizes too short for his frame.

Everyone turned their attention to the back of the room.

Proceeding out of the hallway was Patsy, wearing lots of makeup, but looking absolutely ravishing, as she slowly sashayed in her mother's wedding dress. Accompanying her out of the hallway and then down the aisle was Redfield, who towered over her. I didn't know the big guy very well, but he apparently watched Patsy for years for her father and they had developed a strong bond.

Ron had volunteered for the job, but he already had a commitment. So I was happy when Patsy announced she had someone who really knew her and could stand in for her father.

The moment Patsy began walking down the aisle, Joey's face lit up. It was obvious he still had feelings for her and was genuinely happy to be where he was right now.

Joey turned his head slightly toward Compton, who whispered something to him, and they both laughed. I was going to have to ask them to share the joke.

When Patsy reached the front of the room, she let go of Redfield. She stopped to face Joey, offering him a brilliant smile. He leaned into her and kissed her on her cheek.

Then he stepped to the other side of the two unlit candles.

Patsy now completely focused her attention on Compton, who stepped forward and took her hand. With her other hand, she lightly swiped Compton's newly shaven chin and mouthed, "For me?" He smiled and nodded in response. They both then turned toward the guests.

Everyone eagerly turned back again to wait for the next bride.

I don't think I had seen Chloe Evens radiate more beauty than she did at that moment. She wore Suzie Halston's wedding gown, which wasn't tight fitting like Patsy's, but worked out better as it mostly hid her advanced pregnancy. Truly, on this day, she would have appeared gorgeous in a paper sack. In this wedding gown, she looked amazing. Like Patsy, Chloe beamed joy as she marched slowly beside Ron, her arm locked around his.

They proceeded to the front of the room, where Ron kissed Chloe on her cheek and released her hand to Joey.

All eyes were now on the two couples.

Trunk began, "Dearly beloved, we are gathered here..."

After the wedding, Trunk and Suzie held the reception in the same living room. Everyone helped to add tables, around which the seats were rearranged.

Meanwhile, Suzie and Wilma brought out the feast they'd been working on for days. Trunk, besides acting as pastor and officiant, had cooked up a batch of moonshine to ply everybody's already happy spirits. By the second glass, he was telling everyone it was based on one of Bobby McBoyd's family recipes. Wilma told us that she thought it was a great way to, as she put it, "honor some of the good that came out of Bobby's messed-up life."

Everyone seemed to be enjoying themselves. But I couldn't help feel like this was all bittersweet.

"It's going to be hard to leave this behind, isn't it?" Ron asked from his seat beside me.

It was like he was reading my mind, which he seemed to be doing more often these days. But I also knew what was happening tomorrow weighed heavy on his mind as well.

"It feels like we are already home now," I said. "But I know we'll make Blackstone feel like a home too."

"I'm hoping that we'll make a difference in their community, just like we already have here," Ron said.

"And..." Leticia added. "They can't wait to listen to my audio book of our stories." She smiled widely. She had spent some time editing and organizing her recordings, she said like a book, so as to use it as our audio resume. Blackstone had warned us that their entrance procedure would include several interviews, but that her audio book would minimize that necessity.

Shortly after Bobby's death, Wilma had turned over our supplies, including Leticia's logbook, our maps, and the shortwave transceiver which Bobby's men had taken from the RV. Shortly after this, Leticia was making weekly contact with Blackstone. Each time, they expressed interest in our joining them. It was obvious they wanted Ron the most of us. His unique skillset, only helped by his time here, was desperately needed since their power also came from geothermal vents in Yellowstone.

"I..." Bigelow cut in, "just can't wait to get to one of the two restaurants in my bunker and start eating some real food." He made a show of dropping his fork into his partially eaten food.

I ignored his comment and kept my attention on Leticia, who sat next to him. She rolled her eyes at his comment. She had also made radio contact with the administrators of Bigelow's bunker complex in Colorado and confirmed that Bigelow was in fact alive and coming to his luxury condo, with some guests. They also said they were looking for a few people with skills.

Ron pointed out that dropping off Bigelow wouldn't be much of a diversion before our getting to our final destination. Personally, I was just looking forward to not having to hear Bigelow's insufferably high-pitched voice anymore. Every utterance from him was like 10-inch nails on a chalkboard.

Behind Bigelow, Compton was hand-in-hand with his new bride, walking toward us.

I waved and assumed they were making their rounds from table to table, as was tradition and insisted upon by Suzie.

"Hello Eugene and Patsy," I announced with a grin. During the ceremony we finally learned Compton's first name was Eugene. I couldn't wait to poke some fun at him since the whole time, he'd been hiding his full name from us.

As expected, not even a sly grin from him. Instead, he glanced over his shoulder, then back at us and said, "We need to talk."

When I saw Joey and Chloe were approaching from behind them, and they too weren't smiling, I knew this wasn't going to be good.

"Yes," said Chloe, "we all have an announcement to... make." Her eyes welled up again and immediately started leaking, as they had been during most of their wedding ceremony. Only these were tears of sadness.

"Um," said Joey, whose own eyes were glassy, his voice cracking. "We've all decided to stay here. Chloe and me at the Halstons'; Compton and Patsy at the McBoyds'.

CHAPTER 41

Ron

The day we were equally excited to embrace, as we were dreading, arrived.

Our vehicle was already packed with enough supplies to last us at least a month, even though the trip to Colorado and then to Wyoming should not take any longer than a few days. Even if we had to snowplow our entire way there. Likewise, we had more than enough gas on us to get us there and back.

It was something Compton said: "Whatever you plan for, double it and you'll be half right."

When we were planning this trip for all of us, we were going to go in Bigelow's RV, which had been fixed up and was all ready to go. But when it turned out to be just the four of us and Dog, it didn't make sense to waste all the gas that the RV would suck up. So we opted for our tried and true Landcruiser.

We had just finished saying our goodbyes to the McBoyd family and then to our gracious hosts, the Halstons.

Trunk, after shaking my hand said, "You know this is your home too, Ron. Yours, Nan's and Leticia's. And I'm not just saying that because of your skills."

"Thank you, Trunk, but you know we have to drop off Bigelow. We've made him wait long enough."

"I meant after that... Instead of going to a new place, to people who you don't know and who don't know you... Besides, I've kind of grown attached to having you all here. And so has Suzie."

It was a hard call. But we were like a snowball rolling downhill, picking up more snow, growing larger and gathering speed until it was an unstoppable avalanche. We were determined to make it all the way to Wyoming. The three of us had talked about it extensively. And now we were equally unstoppable in our pursuit, allowing nothing to get in our way. We were going to get there no matter what...

But then we had also planned extensively on the rest of our group coming. Joey and Chloe's staying shouldn't have been a surprise to us. And neither should Compton, after declaring that he was marrying Patsy. But now, and after Trunk's insistence, I had to admit, I wasn't entirely sure.

Is this what Nan and Leticia really want? I began asking myself. It wasn't just my decision; I needed to ask them. Again.

"Thank you, Trunk," I said loud enough that they could hear me. "But the decision is not just mine. It's up to these two, and I would only stay if both Nan and Leticia decided to stay.

"Seriously?" Nan said, cocking her head and glaring at me like I had lost my marbles. "Would you want to deny us our great adventure to Yellowstone?"

"Don't forget, Ronald," Leticia added with an equally puzzled look, "they have that group of young scientists like me, who are studying data to determine what our future might look like. Just like my father, I could be part of a think tank that solves the world's problems."

"I guess we're still going to Yellowstone." Nan hugged Trunk. "Thank you for everything. We will always consider this our home, though. You and Suzie are amazing."

"Thank you, my darling," Trunk said. "Our feelings about you three are the same."

Dog barked, almost as if he wanted to be included.

"You too, Dog," Suzie said, attempting to hold back a smile.

Dog barked again, but this time at Millie, the McBoyds' Shepherd, who also appeared to be there to see us off.

"Don't screw up," said Compton after punching my arm. "And always rely on—"

"—I know, always rely on my team," I replied. "I will not forget that, or you." I offered my hand.

"Don't go all misty on me, Ronald." He gave me a stiff shake and then turned to Leticia, who was glaring at her feet.

"You make sure these two don't get lost, you mad genius." Compton ruffled Leticia's head like he might have done to a little boy.

Leticia wrapped both her arms around him. "You take care of these good people, and don't go all Ted Kaczynski and blow stuff up anymore, you crazy survivalist." She sniffled but didn't let go, holding him tight, until Compton gave her a warm squeeze back.

"I will, kiddo," he said.

They both released at the same time, pretending to be unaffected by their emotional exchange. In a humorous display, Leticia threw her shoulders back and crossed her arms, doing a perfect mimic of Compton, who was doing the same. Those two had built a surprising friendship over the past several months.

"I'll miss your clever repartee, Eugene," said Nan, suppressing a giggle.

Compton accepted a hug from her. "I'm going to miss you, one of the most bad-ass women I have ever had the pleasure of meeting."

Patsy, who had just exchanged goodbyes with Nan and me, punched Compton on the shoulder. "You told me I was the most bad-ass woman you'd ever met."

Compton turned to his wife. "No dear, I was just speaking about my view of you when you walked away."

She punched him again and they both laughed.

"Ronald, brother, it's been a pleasure," Joey said, offering his hand for a shake.

I ignored his hand and chose to bear-hug him instead. "I'm going to miss you, brother," I told him, trying to restrain my own emotions.

"Damn, this is hard," Nan said beside me, her arms tangled around Chloe. They were both crying. "You've grown into quite an awesome person, Chloe Evans."

"You mean two people," Chloe said, tapping her belly. She worked at a smile, but it fell away, and she embraced Nan again.

"We're going to stay in touch," Nan insisted, sounding as if she were regaining some control over her tears. "Remember, we'll check back in with you once a week, using the radio system Leticia set up for the Halstons."

"I know. But it won't be the same..." The floodgates to her eyes opened up again. "I had hoped you would be a part of our baby's life."

That was it. Nan began bawling again.

"Are we going to get going or what?" hollered Bigelow out the rear window, his voice like that of a dying bird.

"I guess His Royal Highness wants to get going," I said. "And he's probably right, as I want to get some mileage in today."

We let go of our friends and drove away, continuing our waving, even as their images shrank away to nothing in our mirrors.

OPPIDUM

CHAPTER 42

Leticia

"Wake me when we get there," Bigelow announced after we left the Halstons'. He snatched one of the blankets, expanding it so that it covered him head to toe, and then acted as though he was going to sleep.

"Good," Nan announced. "We'll wake you in seven days." She was being facetious because that was Ron's 'worst-case estimate' for travel time. We thought it would be more like four days. Thankfully, we were all wrong.

A muffled but meek "I heard that" leaked from the blanket. Until the end, it was one of the few times he spoke the entire trip. Not that any of us were complaining, mind you.

Then there was the snoring.

Moments after his comment to uncountable hours later, the man snored. And snored. And snored some more. His snoring blended in with the other constant sounds of our trip: the whooshing of the shovel pushing the snow away, the grinding noise when it skidded across ice and gravel, and the racket of the truck's tires constantly compacting snow mile after mile.

This was how hours blended into the next day, and then the next, as we drove continuously, only stopping to change drivers, to relieve ourselves, or fill the tank. After each stop, the noises started up again, with Bigelow's snoring topping them all. At some point near the end of the trip, because it was so noisy all the time, I realized Bigelow had stopped snoring for a while. So I asked, "Should we check to see if he's stopped breathing?"

Nan answered, "We'll know soon enough when we eat."

My first thought... Eww! What if he died there? I'd be sitting right next to a dead man... Though actually, he was in between Dog and me. Not that that thought was any less disgusting.

Next thought: What would we do with him if he died? I dozed off thinking about this pressing issue. And this turned into a nightmare where we ran out of food and we were starving to death, so we had to eat Bigelow. I woke up just as Ronald was asking me, "Can you pass me a leg?"

I turned to look at Bigelow, who was sitting up and alert, staring back at me with his eyes which were too close to his pointy nose. "You were having a bad dream," Bigelow said. "Then you mumbled, 'pass me a leg' and I thought, I'd like to eat a leg too, because I'm hungry."

I pictured Ronald gnawing on Bigelow's leg and even though it should have grossed me out, I started laughing. And not just a little. I laughed hysterically, like I was the crazy person in the car. And I went on for an excruciatingly long period of time. But for some reason, I just couldn't stop.

"What's so funny, Teesh?" Nan asked from the driver's seat. I stopped laughing and did a double-take at her.

It wasn't because she switched places with Ronald after I fell asleep and was now driving. It was because only my mother and father called me Teesh. And then recently, Ronald did this too.

"Oh, nothing. Just something Bigelow said which struck me as funny."

"Great," Bigelow said. "I must be here to amuse you." He gave me a smug grin and then turned to face the back of Ronald's head. "Speaking of our jobs, who is the one who's supposed to feed us next? I'm hungry!"

Dog sat up at that. And my stomach grumbled in response. So I guess I was hungry as well.

"You hungry?" Ronald asked Nan, completely ignoring Bigelow.

I could see Nan eyeball Bigelow in the rearview mirror. I knew what she was thinking, because I was thinking it too: Do I hold out eating now just to mess with Bigelow or do I agree to getting out the food so that everyone can eat?

Her mouth opened. Then closed. Then opened again. "Yeah, I'm hungry too."

"At least someone listens to me around here," he whined.

I pulled out another group of the pre-made meals provided by Suzie Halston. This one was pork sandwiches, with her amazing bread. Mine was heavenly. It got me to wondering if they had pork in Wyoming, among some of the other delicacies grown and prepared by the Halstons.

Bigelow, of course, immediately berated his sandwich as being dry and tasteless. But that didn't stop him from devouring every morsel. Then, even though no one asked, he proceeded to tell us more about his bunker condo in Colorado. He went on and on about the heated swimming pool and recreational room, with video games and an endless database of movies. And the food...

lobster—which I couldn't imagine would be replenished anytime soon, because we were in an Ice Age and it was Colorado—and a whole host of other foods he was looking forward to, all prepared by their French chef...

I don't know how long he droned on, because I went to sleep again, as the man continued boasting, in his screechy voice, about all he was going to enjoy.

I woke when Dog pawed me.

"This is it," Bigelow stated.

In front of us was a tall chain-link fence, with barbed wire on top. The fence spread out from both sides, as far as I could see, surrounding a compound of elevated concrete buildings.

"Impressive, isn't it?" Bigelow asked me.

It was, but I wasn't going to give him the satisfaction. "How many... You know, condos in the place?"

"Well, it once was an Army base, before it was bought and then redeveloped as a doomsday bunker for the wealthy. When I last checked months ago, they had sold fifty, but there are at least one hundred condos total. I got in early and bought one of the cheap ones for three-point-four..." I'm guessing he was speaking about millions of dollars, as in three-point-four million dollars. "But the biggest, which the developer kept for himself, was ten times that. He's some Hispanic dude who controls a lot of property in the US."

"Here's my card. You'll need it for the gate." Bigelow passed Ronald, who was now driving, what looked like a black credit card. Bigelow pointed ahead. "Just drive up to the gate and flash the card over the card reader and the gate will open. We'll drive about another half a mile or so and we'll be met at the main gate. The guards will search the vehicle before letting us pass."

He looked back at me, because he assumed I was the only one listening, which was probably true.

"Anyway, what was I saying... Oh yeah, the main guy. I never met him, but I guess he has a few billion bucks, and he's a big guy... He has a moniker about how he looks, but I don't remember what it was. Though it probably doesn't matter, because we'll never meet the guy. But you'll meet the others who are here, none of who I know."

"You mean whom," I interrupted, I think just to be a pain.

"What?"

"The proper English is 'none of whom I know' and not who."

Bigelow scowled at me and continued. "Most of the people who bought here did so quietly, through dummy corporations—that's right, Ronny." Bigelow stopped his narration to instruct Ronald, who had rolled down his driver's side window, thrust out his arm into the cold and waved the card across a tilted card reader. A speaker squeaked, "Welcome home, Mr. Bigelow. Proceed to the next gate." The metal wire gate slid open with a clatter.

"Music to my ears," Bigelow said.

Ronald handed the card back to Bigelow and then proceeded forward, following a newly plowed road—the first we'd found in our two-and-a-half-day journey here—until we came to another gate. This one was made of steel, and overall, much more formidable than the first. It was at least twenty feet tall and bounded on both sides by sloping concrete walls of equal height.

I couldn't even see the top of them immediately in front of us from my back seat.

"As I was saying, many of the people who bought here did so in complete anonymity because, well, they have questionable backgrounds. Mostly bankers and mutual fund billionaires, but others who amassed their wealth from other not so legal means and who don't want their trophy wives or the government knowing where they hid their assets."

Dog barked and his hackles went up. And I could see why.

Five men, dressed in winter camo uniforms, each with automatic weapons, surrounded our vehicle.

"Consequently," Bigelow continued. "They have a lot of security here. They're going to want to interview each of you. But based on your skills, if you want, you'll probably be allowed to stay here. However, if you want to continue to that place in Wyoming, after they're sure you're not a threat to them, they'll let you go on your way."

Bigelow stepped out of the back seat with his hands up. "I'm Steven Bartholomew Bigelow. I own condo number A109. My pin code is Bigelow as in as in Bravo, 1-2-3-4."

What an idiot, I thought.

He ducked down toward Nan's window. "Good luck. I'll see you when they release you."

"Get out of the vehicle with your hands up and surrender your weapons."

I remember thinking then, perhaps we made a big mistake. None of us had any idea, until days later, how big a mistake this could have been.

CHAPTER 43

Ron

Seven days later the door to what essentially was my jail cell opened.

"Hello, Ronald Ash," said the well-dressed man in the doorway with a thick German accent. He looked up from a tablet he was examining. "Helmut Leffler, Director of Security at Oppidum - Colorado. You and your friends have been given acceptance to stay here and are free to move around the complex. Let me show you around and then to where you'll be living. Your friends are there now."

"Oppidum?" I asked. Though I wanted to ask if this one was designated "Colorado," where were the other Oppidum bunkers?

He beckoned me to come out. "It is a Latin word, referring to an important settlement in a Roman administration. But it also refers to the settlement being self-sufficient and fortified against any outside enemy."

"Outside enemy?" I asked.

"Oppidum is fortified and well protected, Mr. Ash. So you and your friends don't have to worry about what's going on outside our walls. Now let me show you why you should feel very lucky to have passed our rigorous screening process to live here. That is, unless you happen to have several million dollars to buy your way in, as did the fifty-six very wealthy owners and their families."

He walked me through a long and narrow concrete hallway, weakly lit by emergency lights, while he told me about Oppidum. Our footsteps echoed as he explained how since the ashfall had started they had many show up at their gates, requesting entry. Often friends of owners, as in our case. But most were rejected and expelled from the compound. However, over several months since the apocalypse, they'd found a need for skilled workers, many of whom were hired by Oppidum but never made it to their complex.

Evidently, this was where we came in. We had been allowed to stay because we could play a role in making sure, as he said, "our complex runs like clockwork."

Then he added something that gave me pause. "Plus, our founder, who gave you final approval, insists on meeting all of you."

"Will we meet him now?" I asked.

"No. He's not here yet. But we're in constant communication. And we expect him within a week or so."

We stopped at an elevator. While we waited, I asked, "How many owners and their family live here versus, whatever we are called... workers?"

"Guests. You are called guests. Though yes, we would expect some work from each of you to stay here. There are currently forty-eight owners with their family members and sixty-five guests, which includes me and our security personnel."

The elevator opened and Helmut pressed the G button on the panel. A female voice with a British accent announced, "Going up." There were five other buttons above that, numbered one through five. There were many buttons below that, including B-105, the floor we were on.

As the door slid shut and we immediately shot upward, I wanted to ask if that meant we were one-hundred and five floors below ground level, or if the number had some other relevance. But when five seconds passed and B-95 lit momentarily, confirming my initial thought, I asked instead, "So, only forty-eight owners and their family? I thought you said fifty-six owners and their family were here."

Helmut studied me with his discerning eyes. It was only a second, but it was enough to tell me that this one watched and listened to everything. "Fifty-six out of one hundred and one condos were sold. But only twenty owners have shown up. Many owners came without spouse or girlfriend, and only two with their children. All grown."

B-55 lit momentarily, followed by B-45.

"Therefore, you will get to enjoy more of the facilities than if we were at full capacity."

We slowed and then a soft tone and the British woman's voice announced, "Ground floor." The door swished open.

"Welcome to Oppidum," Helmut said.

We stepped out into a five-story atrium that resembled a tropical forest, with a water fall noisily cascading down into a pool of water that branched out as little streams, like veins, each shooting around the large open space. The entire football field-sized area was covered in green and flowering plants. Some, like the trees, telescoped up almost thirty feet.

As we stepped into the vast jungle, where the canopy of green opened up, I could better see the atrium's setup. Two ends were lined with balconies, some of them occupied. On the other two sides, a network of glass and steel rose upward, converging into a dome in the middle, giving residents a view of the outside world. The whole thing reminded me of an atrium on one of those mega cruise ships.

There were voices calling out my name and I searched to find them and saw two shapes waving at me. They were on the other side of the atrium, standing on a fourth-floor balcony. It was Nan and Leticia.

I waved back.

"Your lady friend and the child are in your suite now," Helmut said. "But let me show you the rest of the complex first."

"What about my dog?"

"It's being held in our animal area, under quarantine. It should be released soon."

My tour continued throughout the whole ground floor, where he showed me the vast number of rooms and described the services which were attached to them. Then he showed me some of the behind-the-scenes areas, such as their storehouse of food and the machinery which ran everything on B-1 through B-5.

After an hour of this, I came to understand the sheer magnitude of this complex, and I was only being shown a small part of the overall complex.

It was all very impressive. But the entire time, I kept thinking that there was something much more to what Helmut was telling us. First, we never said we were staying, although Bigelow did tell us more than once that we could. But the hands-on exclusive tour by the head of security, including the back end of things, just seemed a little too much.

If they were trying to convince us to stay, because they needed my skills or those of Nan or Leticia, why did they keep us locked up for seven days? And why was I separated from Nan and Leticia this entire time? And why did this mysterious founder want to meet me?

There were too many red flags sprouting up. Any one of them was concerning. All of them were terrifying.

So I asked him what to me was the most important question. "Since we're all good, then you'd have no problem if we got back into our car and left right now, right?"

Helmut looked at me and gave an obviously practiced smile. "Not yet. I want you to take a few days to consider all that we offer before you decide. And as I said, our founder wants to meet all of you when he gets here."

In other words, we are still prisoners here, I thought.

I thanked Helmut for the tour, but I asked if I could see my friends now.

He was gracious and walked me to another elevator, which he said led us to "our suite," as he called it.

On the way up, he handed me a gold Rolex watch. "Please wear this at all times. Besides telling time, it gives us the details of where you are in the complex."

One more huge red flag.

As we exited, Helmut stopped just outside of the elevator, consulted his tablet again and said, "One last item, before I let you go. Your sponsor, Mr. Bigelow, would like to meet you at 13:30 in the main dining room for lunch."

A quick flick of my wrist and my new watch told me it was 12:45. I assumed it was PM, based on the daylight coming through the atrium earlier.

He walked me to an entrance door. "This is your suite. Let us know if you need anything." He turned around and walked back into the elevator and disappeared.

The solid-looking door, which Helmut said was made of two-inch steel, had decorative tiles that revealed its address: B405. On each side of the entrance were two potted ficus trees. Like this place, they were too perfect to be real.

I knocked and announced myself. The door flew open. Nan swarmed the doorway and threw her arms around me. So did Leticia.

After our long embraces, I noticed that each of them also wore Rolex watches.

CHAPTER 44

Leticia

"They think we're living here now? And we thought we'd never see you," Nan spoke in a rapid-fire succession of sentences. "Are you okay? Come inside so we can talk. I really nee—"

Ronald put his finger to Nan's lips, telling Nan to quit speaking. Then he pointed to his ears and pointed to the ceiling.

He thinks the place is bugged.

Nan was about to speak again, but I too put my finger to my lips and shook my head.

Ronald walked into the luxury condo's foyer. He halted abruptly when the robotic vacuum came out of its caddy and shot toward the kitchenette to begin its sweeping. It must have sensed the food Nan had dropped when she heard Ronald's knock at the door.

Ronald ignored the machine's buzz across the floor, as he proceeded into the living room, and then toward the balcony. His head pivoted from side to side, up and down as he walked... He was searching for something.

I knew what he wanted, and I knew where he could find it too. I flagged him down and led Ronald and Nan out to the balcony and closed the sliding doors behind us.

We were now out in the atrium areas, which were a clatter of sounds: the waterfall crashing below, piped-in birds chirping, the whoosh of faux breezes, and the mumble of others speaking. "I think it's safe out here from bugs," I said. I didn't know this, but it made sense that if they had set up a listening device in the place, they would be focused on areas where they could hear clear conversations. And it would be harder to hear them out here.

Ronald nodded but didn't say anything. He took his watch off and motioned for us to do the same. We did and he deposited them in a pile, just inside, before rejoining us on the balcony.

The words burst from his lips, but as whispers. "First, are you both doing all right? They didn't hurt you?" His head turned to Nan and then me.

"I'm fine," I said. "But I fear it's my fault they held you so long."

Ronald cocked his head. "Why would you think that?"

"Because I gave them our audio recordings, after they began interviewing me—you know, like Bigelow said they would. So I told them that we recorded everything leading up to here. I figured that if they heard how resourceful we were and that we helped one of their owners, that they would help us get to our final destination in Wyoming..." I felt a shot of embarrassment and looked away from Ronald.

"I think I oversold us and now they want us to stay... After that, they didn't ask me any more questions. They just gave me food and my books—those that the Halstons gave me—but I had to stay in my room until today."

Ronald's eyes dripped compassion. "Your recordings are not why they held us. In fact, Helmut Leffler, the head of security, told me we were lucky to have passed their screening. But there is a lot more to this than they're saying."

He turned his head to Nan. "You all right?"

She nodded. "Fine also. Other than the confinement, they've been wonderful hosts to us."

"Too good, I'd say," Ronald continued at a whisper. "I mean, look at this place." He spread his arms out toward the atrium. "And especially this." He pointed toward the inside of the condo. "Bigelow said he got one of the bargain suites on the ground floor; that most of the others—which I'm guessing would include this one—were more than the three-plus-million he paid for his. And they're letting us stay here? Why? For a little work in exchange for our boarding here?"

"I know," Nan said. "Completely agree they are hiding some big secrets. For instance, why haven't they given us Dog yet?"

Ronald nodded. "They said he'll be out of quarantine soon."

"They told us that too," Nan said. "Also, I chatted up our housekeeper just minutes before you arrived."

"You mean one of the... guests?" Ronald made air quotes with his fingers when he said guests.

Nan looked a little confused and then her eyes sprang to life. "Right, all of us non-owners are called guests. Anyway, the housekeeper let slip that the other guests"—Nan also made exaggerated air quotes—"live somewhere in the basement floors. Weirder still, after she said this to me, she got very nervous. She spun around, as if she thought someone were behind her... listening. Then she abruptly excused herself and left."

Nan then pointed to the pile of our newly gifted watches on the other side of the sliders. "And then there's that. I've never received a Rolex watch at any place I've ever stayed. Much less a gold one."

Ronald nodded acknowledgment. "Do you have anything on the founder of this place?"

"Only that that's his place." Nan pointed straight across the vast open area and up one floor, to the balcony that took up the whole fifth floor of the A condos. "And that he has not yet shown up but is expected soon."

Ronald stared at the balcony but didn't say anything. His face was twisted with worry, and I wished I knew why. "Yeah, supposedly he's aware of our case and he wants to meet all of us in person after he arrives."

"Are we still leaving this place and going to Blackstone?" I asked. "This place is beautiful and all, but it's kind of creepy, they have few books in their library, and I'd just as soon get going to Wyoming."

"Assuming we're allowed to leave, that is," Nan said.

Ronald reacted to a thought and made a quick movement for the slider. He slipped in, looked at the largest of the watches and left it in the pile, returning. "I've got to go," he said, his voice almost impossible to hear. I leaned closer and so did Nan. "Bigelow asked to meet me in about ten minutes. I'm going see if I can dig for more information on this place, about the founder and our being able to leave when we want. Meanwhile, you two split up and explore how we get outside and where our car and supplies might be. And find out where Dog is being held."

He looked around and then leaned in close to both of us and kept his voice low. "And be careful about what you say to each other and to others. Consider that everything you say is probably being listened to."

"I'm scared," I said. I hated admitting to it. But I was scared. I didn't know what was going on, though like Ronald and Nan, I knew there was more to this place than we were hearing.

"Oh, honey." Nan hugged me. "Don't worry. We got into this together. We'll get out of this. Together."

Ronald put his hand on my shoulder and attempted a reassuring smile.

I knew I could do this, with both of them.

"All right," Ronald said, still whispering. "I will meet you back here in a couple of hours."

CHAPTER 45

Ron

The so-called Main Dining Room was fancier than anything I had eaten in before.

The Maître d' saw me approaching, glanced at a tablet like the one that Helmut carried, and said, "Greetings, Mr. Ash. Your party is waiting for you at one of our best tables." I glared at my watch, connecting the fact that every one of Oppidum's staff who carried these tablets could see where every one of their owners and guests were at every moment, so long as they wore one of their watches. I'm sure the owners were sold on getting more personalized service and better protection, not realizing it was at the cost of their freedom.

"Hey there, Ronny," hollered the voice that would make paint peel.

"Stevie," I said, attempting to be just as annoying by matching his tone. But more than being annoyed, I was angry: This man got us into this mess. And he damned well was going to help us get out of it too.

"Sit. I ordered you a shot of their best tequila—Hey, you got one of these things too?" He made a show of the matching gold Rolex dangling from his scrawny wrist. "Usually, they give the cheaper digital jobs to the guests. You must have friends in high places." He grinned widely and thrust his shot glass filled with amber colored liquid into the air. But rather than slamming it back like one would usually drink a shot, he sipped at its edges lightly, with his pinky extended.

My urge to punch this man was as strong as ever. However, I needed answers and I needed him on my side to get us out. Add to this the complication of not being able to ask anything without knowing who was listening.

I had an idea.

Sticking my wrist out, I conspicuously removed my new watch and laid it carefully on the table. "I need to go to the restroom. Escort me there."

He gave me a vacant gaze, obviously not understanding. So I leaned in and whispered, "Lose the watch, stand up and walk with me." Then I saw it in his eyes.

Fear.

Steve Bigelow must be afraid of what my request might mean to him and his lifestyle here. I could only guess what Helmut and those in charge of the place said to him while we were being held.

He nodded, shoulders slumping, certainly resolving that this was something he had to do. He stood from his table, leaving his watch on his seat, and headed for the back of the restaurant.

A waiter arrived just as I left and passed by. "Restroom," I announced behind me, and I followed behind Bigelow.

Once inside the men's room and confirming it was empty, I turned on all the faucets and signaled for Bigelow to come closer.

When he was close enough that only he would hear me, assuming the restrooms were bugged too, I stuck my face directly in front of his and I let him have it. "You realize we are captives here, because of you. "My index finger was a dagger point, thrust into his chest. "And I want to know why we were given a luxury condo to quote-unquote live in, which is better than yours. I know you didn't do this, so who's pulling the levers and why?"

The tears started immediately. "I'm sorry. It wasn't me... I-I don't have any more power here than you."

He grabbed a handful of tissues from a dispenser and blew loudly. "I don't know why they're so interested in your group. When we arrived, I told them that you were my friends and that you all had useful skills and that maybe they could give you a job and make you an offer to stay... I mean, I-I like you guys and didn't want you to leave. Bu-but I didn't think they would keep you locked up for seven days."

"Is that all you said to them?" I asked, now more puzzled than ever at what was happening to us. I was sure that Bigelow knew what was going on. But it appeared now that he didn't. He sucked at lying. So I was pretty sure he was telling me the truth.

"No. The next day, they said that they listened to your tapes or something, and they had more questions. Then they said..." His eyes got more watery. "They knew we weren't really good friends, that you were taking me here only because of the deal that we made, and that you didn't really like me—which hurt, by the way." He blew again into his tissue wad.

"Then they grilled me about what I knew about your time in Texas."

"Texas?" I asked because that didn't make sense.

"It seemed weird to me too, because I would have thought that what you did at that ranch was more important than what you did before."

He tossed his used tissues in the wastebasket and grabbed another handful, blotting at his face, like a woman would do with her makeup.

Really, I was analyzing everything he said and what I knew, in an attempt to figure out why we were not allowed to leave. It had to lead to the person who was in charge, whomever that was.

"So who is this founder you mentioned, who owns the fifth floor and runs this place?"

Fear flashed back onto his face. "Um..." He looked for more tissues. Seeing that he emptied the box already, he reached for another one by the last sink.

I grabbed his arm before he could slink over there and waste more time we probably didn't have. "Answer the damned question!"

His eyes locked into mine. They flitted around, trying to escape like a trapped animal. "It's a wealthy businessman. You might actually know him because he owns a lot in Texas." His eyes tried desperately to pull away from mine, but I squeezed so hard, my hand began hurting me.

"Ow... I told you I couldn't remember his name. But I do..."

I squeezed even harder.

"His name is Hector Morales, but he goes by the name Polar Bear."

CHAPTER 46

Nan

It was far worse than I could ever have imagined. I had such difficulty finding my breath, I had to stop several times on the jog back to our lodging at B405.

Hector Morales AKA El Oso Polar or Polar Bear?

I thought we put him and his band of murderous crazies behind us after we ditched Trout. So how was it possible that he had found us after all this time? How was it possible that we just happened to stumble upon the same place that Polar Bear owned and ran, after running from him for months?

Not again I thought. Once more, Perdition, as Suzie Halston called it, struck. Eternal punishment for all of my past sins.

At the elevator, I seriously thought I would pass out from not taking in enough air. But when it dinged, something snapped inside me.

I took in a deep breath and stood up tall. The British voice told me I was going up, and I told it, "Damn right I am."

It was something I realized through all of our trials and tribulations. That I wasn't the cause of the wrongs of the world, no matter the severity of my own wrongs. It was evil people that caused our afflictions, not a vengeful God.

Evil people were going to do what they do, whether I was doing something sinful or not. Further, I found out that I could depend on others, like my new family. Last, it was Suzie who helped me to see that it wasn't just my own strength, or that of others; it was God.

When the door slid open, my hands were already locked and I was giving thanks for Ron and Leticia and Dog, and Him.

I knew then and there we would find some way out of this. I just didn't know how yet. But He would help all of us find it. I was sure of it.

Leticia

Once more, I got my recordings back.

And it was all because of a boy named Alfred Leffler.

I was roaming the halls, looking for our escape out of this place. I checked the handle of a door to see if it was locked and it opened on its own.

"Oh, hi!" said the surprised German teenager. He glanced at my wristwatch and then beamed a huge smile. "I'm Alfred Leffler. You must be with the new people."

I remembered his last name from Ronald's description of Helmut, who I presumed was his father.

"Hi, I'm Leticia... Hey, isn't your father the HMFIC of this place?"

When he laughed, I knew I liked him. "Yes, he's head of security. Was your family in the military?"

Impressive that he knew about the acronym's origins...

Stick to the mission, Leticia.

"No. I just read a lot... Especially electronics books and books on how things work. You know, "back of the curtain" kind of things?"

"Oh, then you'll need to come with me. Let me show you some things you won't get on the usual welcome-to-your-doomsday-home tour of the place."

"Cool," I said. I knew I probably was going to go overboard with my words of encouragement. And I immediately felt guilt for what I was about to do, but I knew I was up against the clock, and I really wanted to get out of here. "Alfred," I said softly. "I had no idea I'd find a cute boy who liked the same things I do here."

Alfred turned a bright shade of crimson. He grabbed my hand and then said, "Come on."

We ran to a stairwell at the end of the hallway. He waved his watch by a touch pad to the right of the lock and the lock disengaged. He shined a proud smile. "Father doesn't know that I know how to program their watches so that I can go anywhere in the complex." We slipped into the stairwell and went down one floor.

"But doesn't he track you too with these things?" I asked, surprised at my luck.

"Nope. Figured that out too." He stopped before we exited the stairwell. "Say, you're right. I need to reprogram yours too, so they can't figure out where you are. First stop, the workshop."

He cracked the door and edged his head in just enough that he could see. After turning both directions, he said, "Okay, coast is clear."

We trotted past two doors with numbers on them to a nondescript door without any markings on it. With a flick of his wrist it clicked open.

Inside was a cramped work area, with electronic devices stacked on top of others and wires everywhere. I lied when I said I liked electronics books. I had to read a few because I wanted to learn how to build a radio, but it wasn't something I got joy out of. Alfred was another story.

He lifted my arm up and stealthily removed my watch, popped the back off and went to work on it, like Julia Child took to a saucepan. Within seconds he had wires connected to parts of its innards, leading to a computer. He tapped away like a writer on deadline. In less than five minutes, he had the watch sealed up and back on my arm.

With a wide grin, he hopped off his seat. "I also gave you access to every door in the complex, just like me. But the best part is when you pull out this button"—he demonstrated on his watch—"and push it back in, the watch will reset to your being in your bed, at your condo, number B405. Security's computers will think you're there until you return and then leave again. Only then will they begin tracking you again."

"That's too cool." And it was. But something Ronald said led me to whisper, "Wait, don't these things have a bug in them too?"

"Nope. No bugs. But they probably do have a bug in your living room. So say whatever you want to there to embarrass them. I mean, what are they going to do to you? You're an owner!"

I just smiled at that one. He didn't know, and I wasn't going to say anything different. It was better that he assumed I was an owner.

"Okay next, you don't mind getting a little dirty, do you?"

"They called me a tomboy back home." Again, I fibbed a little. They really called me a nerd—they meant it to be pejorative, but I never minded—and other things, which were not very nice.

Alfred grabbed my hand and pulled me around a bench to the opposite side of the room and an access panel in the wall. "Now let me show you the security area." He opened up the panel. "We can't go into the control center because there is always someone there. But I can show you something you'll really, really like." Again, he flashed me an adorable grin.

He took me through some ducting, where electric and other heavily shielded wires ran. But the area was almost tall enough for even me to walk in. After a few minutes we arrived at another panel.

He did what many of us were doing today: He held a finger to his lips.

After not hearing anything on the other side, he opened the panel, and we entered a room with a lot of monitors.

“This is the secondary security station. It doesn't have as many monitors as the control station, but it does have something better." He pointed at a wall with lockers, labeled with a letter and number, which appeared to correspond to each condo's number. One of them said B405. "Go ahead and use your watch. As I said, it works on every lock now."

I did and the metal door clicked open. Inside were our bug out bags, and...

"Our BOBs and my satchel?"

Was it possible?

"BOBs?" Alfred asked, but I ignored him.

I opened my satchel and inside were my recorder, logbook, and SD cards. They were all there!

I looked up at Alfred, who once again grinned back. What I did next was spontaneous, because it felt right. I leaned up to Alfred and kissed him on the lips. "Thank you for this."

It was the first time I had kissed a boy. And for the first time that I could remember, I felt alive. Really alive.

"I-I didn't look in there. I just knew that's where they keep the things they don't want you to have when you first check in."

My mind was awash in thoughts and questions. So I tried to focus on what would help us the most. Right now. "Would they know that someone went in here and took something out?"

"Well, they don't go in there, unless you've done something. And because you're cleared, I don't think they'll check it anytime soon."

"What about the vehicle we came in? Is it possible to access it... without getting caught?"

He smiled the same mischievous smile he did when he started our little tour. "Come here." He waddled low, over to the computer screens. "Don't stand up, because they might see you in the next room."

Beyond the computer screens was a window wall. I nodded my understanding.

He slipped up into the chair, sitting in a low slouch. After typing a few keys, he held out his hand and pulled me up high enough to see the images on the screen. "Cool vehicle," he said. "That's yours, right?" He pointed to our Landcruiser, parked on the edge of an indoor parking lot.

I nodded.

"Okay, you'll need to exit out this door..." He pointed on the screen to a door a few feet from the vehicle. "... And you get to that door here." He clicked a key and a new image appeared on the screen. "This is one floor below us, accessible by the same stairwell we came down. Do you remember how to get there?"

I nodded. But then a smirk formed on my face, and I didn't mind that he saw it.

"You'll want to go at midnight. That's when they do shift change. But if you go tonight, will you take me? I can help you."

I didn't know if he understood I wanted to leave this place or if he thought I was doing what I used as the excuse: to get something else from our vehicle and not get caught. Still, I nodded and added, "Of course."

"Okay, it's a date," he said. His smile evaporated in an instant when he checked his watch. "I forgot. I'm supposed to meet my father back at our home right now. So we need to go."

We followed the reverse route silently. He even helped to carry two of our BOBs, saying, "A pretty girl, even if she's a tomboy, shouldn't have to carry all the bags."

Like a gentleman, he walked me back to my door. "Will I see you at midnight?"

I shrugged my shoulders because I honestly didn't know. I kissed him once more and said, "Thank you for everything."

He blushed again and said, "See ya." He dashed for the elevator, as he played with the button on his watch, no doubt to show his father, if he looked on his tablet, where he was then, when it would have said he was at home.

Using my newly programmed Rolex, I flicked my watch at the door and it clicked open.

There I found Ronald and Nan on the balcony talking ear to ear.

CHAPTER 47

Ron

At eleven-fifteen, we were out the door for good... That was if luck cared to shine on us just once more. Trunk would have said, "Blessed."

Whatever it was called, we needed to be pretty richly blessed or pretty damned lucky to pull off what we had planned.

The three of us reviewed my plan, none of which would have come together or had been possible if it weren't for both Nan and Leticia. And truly what Leticia pulled off was mind numbing. We were blessed. So far.

I left my watch in my bed. Nan left hers in her bed. And Leticia manipulated hers, per Leffler's kid, such that the monitors would think she remained in her bed.

At the foot of the door, there was a handwritten note that had Leticia's name on it. She quickly read it and whispered that everything was fine.

We soft-walked down the hall to the stairwell, each of us toting our heavy BOBs—Nan's and mine had our weapons inside them—but not our winter gear. We agreed if we saw anyone on the way down, it would be too hard to explain that. We would have to chance it without.

Quietly, but quickly, we made our way down, and out to the ground floor hallway.

"Howdy neighbor." A man wearing a giant Stetson and a shit-eating grin stood offering a handshake. "I'm Wyatt Cooper, of Dallas, Texas."

I shook his hand firmly. "Ronald or Ron. And this is Nan and Leticia; we're from Hill Country."

"Well, slap my ass and call me Sally. I didn't know we had any other Texans here... Folks can't sleep neither?"

"No, sir," Nan said, in a drawl I had never heard from her. "Thought I'd take my hubs and our daughter out for a run around the atrium. Full pack, naturally." She pivoted so that he could get full view of the over-stuffed backpack. "Care to join us?"

He looked us over, each of us with our equally heavy-looking BOBs on our backs, and he bellowed out a laugh from his rotund belly. "You folks go right ahead. One of these times, let's chew the fat over some steaks and beer at The Grill."

"Look forward to it, Wyatt," I said.

"Bye," Leticia said with a slight a drawl, adding a cherry on top.

Nan led us to our first stop: to pick up Dog.

She had tracked down the same Mexican housekeeper who had revealed previous info. This time, Nan pleaded with the housekeeper to find out how to visit her dog who was still in quarantine. Not only did she give the location, but the fact that the animals were left unattended after eighteen-hundred or 6PM.

Once at the Pet Condos, Leticia passed her Rolex at the door, and it opened. The rest was easy, because there were no humans there, and only five dogs. All but Dog were Chihuahuas. As we led Dog to the exit, I noticed the sign above the door said it all. "No animals beyond this point. All animals must remain in this area. No exceptions."

Now Leticia led us, as she knew the rest of the way.

At a stairwell entrance, she flicked her watch at it and the door unlocked. She slipped in, with us following close behind.

Although we were doing everything to be quiet, each footfall made a much louder clatter than I had hoped. At the Basement level B-2, we stopped at a door, finally enjoying the safety of being quiet. The only sounds were our breathing and Dog's panting.

Leticia whispered, "This door leads to a hall I haven't been on, but supposedly, it leads to the exit where our truck is parked. I'm going to peek and make sure no one is in the hallway." We both nodded in the red glare of the stairwell's emergency lights.

After a few seconds of checking, she said, "Clear," and we were walking briskly down a brightly lit hallway, all the way to its end and hopefully our final door.

We decided I would go first, followed by the others. I so wanted to take out my weapon, but if we had to fire it, there would be no chance we could go any further.

We were out the door and breaking for our vehicle in the darkness of the parking garage. Earlier I had pulled out my spare key that I had kept in my BOB, and got us inside immediately.

Once I was behind the wheel, I glanced at Bigelow's watch, which was so snug on my wrist, it felt like it was cutting off my circulation.

Just one more hurdle, I coaxed myself.

"Okay, it's go time," I said to Nan and Leticia, who were already placing blankets over them and Dog, while they lay on the floor in back.

"Here goes," I said. The truck started right up and we were headed out of the garage, and then to the heavy-duty gate. One guard was on duty, and as I pulled up to him, he gave me a you-don't-belong-here glare.

Once again, I found myself saying a little prayer.

I rolled down the window and he glanced first at his tablet, then at me. "Kind of late to be out for a drive, isn't it, Mr. Bigelow?" He looked back at his tablet then back at me. "And all alone."

It was working exactly as planned. I steadied my breath, amazed that we hadn't had any hitches. He thought I was Bigelow because I was wearing Bigelow's watch. And he didn't know that Nan and Leticia were in back because their watches were not here. At least that's what his tablet said.

I yawned like I meant it. "Hell, yeah. It's way past my bedtime. When those people gave me a ride here seven days ago, they threw some of my stuff out the window, just outside of the fence. I wanted to go retrieve it and then come back."

The guard looked at his tablet again. "Usually, I have to get the okay from someone in Security before I can let anyone leave these premises.

Shit! I hadn't counted on that. Bigelow said he could come and go as he liked. But he said at just before midnight shift change, it shouldn't be a problem. The outgoing guard would not want any complications. However, this guard saying he needed some sort of approval from Leffler was definitely a problem.

The click of Nan's AR pistol in back told me she was ready to fire on this guy, if he pushed it much further. She needed to wait just a moment or two longer: I had to convince the guard to get the gate open first, or we would be stuck here.

"I'll just be on the other side of the big fence out there. Then I'm coming back. Surely you can let an owner get the rest of his belongings," I argued. The back of my neck was sweaty.

We needed to get out of here in the next five minutes, before the new guard came on duty, or we would be stuck here.

The rustle of Nan's blanket told me she was about to stand up and use her weapon.

"Sorry, but I have to call someone. Hey..."

I shot a glance in my rearview mirror but didn't see Nan. I looked over at the guard, who was mouthing words to his tablet.

"Okay, no problem. I just got authorization from Security. You can go and then return. Do you need any assistance, Mr. Bigelow?"

"No. I'll be fine. Thank you."

When I had rolled up the window, Nan blew out a breath. "Damn, I think I peed myself just a little."

"Thank you, Alfred Leffler," Leticia said, her voice low and muffled from under their blanket. "He wanted to leave with us, but his father was watching him too closely. However, in his note, he said he would be watching us remotely and would try and help to 'make things happen if we needed.'"

Thank you, Alfred Leffler, whomever you are, I thought but didn't dare say out loud.

The gate slid open, and we drove forward. Then the gate slid closed, and we continued, at first slowly, then picking up our speed.

"We're out of the main gate," I said. "But stay down until we're outside the complex."

Two muffled "Okays."

As we approached the chain-link gate, it automatically opened and we drove right out. I checked Bigelow's watch again, unclasping it and releasing it in the process. I stopped us just outside the gate. "Okay, you can come out."

Both their heads popped up. So did Dog's.

They watched me as I rolled down the window and tossed Bigelow's watch out into the snow.

"What time is it?" Nan asked.

"It's 12:10," Leticia said.

"Then it's time," I said, looking in my rearview mirror. At that moment, all the lights in the complex went out. "Right on time."

"How did you do that, Ronald?" Leticia asked.

"Our boy has skills," Nan answered. "I'm more impressed that you got Bigelow to give you his watch. Won't they come down on him when they find out he helped us escape?"

"No, I don't think so. He's going to tell them that I stole it."

"Okay, I'll ask the question neither of you want to ask," Leticia said. "What do we do about Polar Bear?"

"Nothing," I said.

"Ronald's right," Nan said, actually calling me Ronald rather than Ron for the first time since we met. "Bigelow was asleep the whole time we left Arizona. So he won't be able to tell anyone how to find Halston's ranch. They should be safe. And as for us, he only knows that we're going to somewhere in Wyoming. He has no clue where that might be. And because Leticia was able to regain possession of her audio, they can't go back and review what they listened to. So no, he won't find us."

They were quiet in the back, probably coming to terms with this the same way I was.

Not long after we started moving outside the gate, I had to lower the shovel, as the snow had already drifted over the road since we passed this way a week ago.

We headed down the same road we came up to find Oppidum, until it connected with I25. I put the truck in park. In front of us were our choices: One sign pointed to a turnoff North, which would take us to Wyoming, and ultimately our final destination, Blackstone. The other sign pointed to the turnoff to the South, taking us back to Arizona and the Halstons' ranch, near Safford.

I turned on the dome light and spun around in my seat to face Nan, Leticia, and Dog.

"Any doubts about where we're going?" I asked, putting both my hands on the seat back.

"None!" Leticia stated emphatically, as she laid a hand on one of mine and squeezed it.

"Nan?"

She radiated a glowing smile, reached over for my other hand, and gave it a squeeze. "Nope. Take us home, Ronald."

"Dog?"

He pawed our arms and woofed.

We laughed at this.

With a giggle still reverberating in my chest, I put the truck in gear and turned right.

CHAPTER 48

Ron

I woke up from another dream about Liz. This time it wasn't a nightmare.

Usually, my dreams about Liz involved death and blood and her telling me that I failed her, that I let her die. But this one was different.

We were on our boat, enjoying a cold beer in the hot sunshine. Liz was in her favorite bathing suit, smiling at me through her beer. Then it started to snow.

The snow grew deep, and I was afraid that Liz would freeze. But she didn't seem worried at all. She stood up resolutely, put down her beer and, still smiling, she walked over to me. She leaned into me and kissed me on the lips—oh, how I missed this—and she whispered in my ear, "It's okay, darling. I want you to be happy. She's a good woman. If you take care of her like you always took care of me, she will be a lucky woman. And don't worry, you'll never forget us and the love we had for each other..."

My eyes were closed as I listened to her speak. But then she stopped speaking.

I knew then she was gone. But I didn't want to open my eyes. Instead, I held onto the image of her, as I heard a familiar George Straight tune playing in the background.

It was about going to Mexico and it was one of Liz's favorites. It was one of a CD of a mix of tunes I'd long since recorded and played on the boat often. But the jostling of the truck reminded me that I was no longer on our boat, or in a dream.

My eyes flicked open to daylight. I turned and saw Nan driving... and singing. Her hands were tapping a beat against the steering wheel, and she was sounding quite nice mimicking George's words.

After a while, she turned to me and said, "What?"

"Oh, nothing," I said.

With one hand, she turned down the CD player's volume. "You're smiling," she said, smiling back. It was genuine and bright, causing her scar to combine with her smile lines, making her seem more... beautiful.

At that moment, I felt something I had not felt for Nan before this, and not for any other woman since Liz... Was it love? I wondered.

Nan held her smile, while glancing at me, eager for some more detail, and then her eyes returned to the road.

"I guess I feel... Happy," I told her. It was true.

"I am too," said Leticia from the back seat.

"Woof," Dog proclaimed.

"Sir Lancelot says he's happy too," Leticia said through her teeth, while leaning on the seat back between me and Nan.

"Sir Lancelot?" Nan asked. "I thought we called him Dog."

"Hope you don't mind, Ronald. It's just that Dog is no name for your noble companion. The one who watches over you and protects you."

"He's as much yours, even all of ours, as he is mine. So I'll bite. Where did that name come from?"

"If you'll recall, Sir Lancelot is from the tale of King Arthur. He was the fearless protector of the king's knights."

"Does that make you his Guinevere?" Nan asked with a giggle.

"I like it," I said.

"Woof," Sir Lancelot added.

"What is it, Sir Lancelot?" Nan asked.

"Woof-woof-woof," he exclaimed, pawing the seat back.

We looked out in the distance and saw McBoyd's blockade. George Halston, Trunk's brother, was there. He was carrying a rifle as one of McBoyd's guards always did. Only this time he wasn't brandishing it. He was waving at us. We pulled up alongside him and Nan lowered her window. "Hey George, what are you doing manning the blockade?"

"Just trying to pay my penance for past sins. And it was my turn on watch."

"Is everything good there?" Nan asked.

"Quite well, thank you. And welcome back. You know they're waiting for you."

"Whoopee!" proclaimed Leticia. "Hi George."

"Hey there, Leticia. How's the writing coming along?"

"Great! You're in my first book and so are both families."

"Oh-oh, hope you're not going to kill me off."

"No." Leticia shined her don't-be-ridiculous face. "It's kind of nonfiction. So it turns out well for you."

"Good to hear. Can't wait to read it. Now you folks better get moving. Temps are dropping today, and I can smell snow flurries coming. Besides, they have a surprise for you. Also, Wilma will want you over for dinner soon. Then you can see how our growing operations have... blossomed, thanks to all of you!"

"Sounds great, George. We'll see you soon." Nan rolled up the window, put us in gear and we headed to the ranch.

The clouds ahead were turning darker, and it did look like another snowstorm was coming, as George suggested. But these clouds didn't feel ominous anymore. In fact, there was no anxiety about what lay ahead for us. Only excitement. Yes, it was going to be brutal living through another ice age which could last as long as we were alive. God willing, it'd be a long life.

But for the first time since I lost Liz, I felt hope for what lay ahead. I was looking forward to the future.

"We're almost home and I can hardly wait," said Leticia.

I grinned at this, and I'm sure it was from ear to ear. It was the first time I heard Leticia refer to anyplace as her home.

"What do you suppose the surprise is?" Nan asked.

I shot a sly grin at Nan and she at me. We already knew what the surprise was, or rather surprises. Joey had told us on Leticia's ham radio when we had made contact yesterday to tell them of our trip. But we wanted what we were about to see to be a surprise for Leticia. So we kept mum about it.

"You two already know?" Leticia asked, glancing at me and then Nan and then back, trying to gain something from our expressions. "Well, it must be good then, if you haven't told me. I can't wait."

In the distance, we could see a group of people standing in the middle of the road. We couldn't really make out their faces, but we knew who they were.

"It's them!" Leticia shouted, now standing up from her seat.

"It sure is," Nan said. "I'm excited too."

"Woof-woof-woof," Sir Lancelot barked, also in excitement. Running up the drive was Millie, who was McBoyd's dog but had been staying at the Halstons' for a reason.

"Yes, Sir Lancelot, that's Millie." Leticia petted him. "I wonder if Millie's pups have come?"

I just smiled.

"Is that the surprise?"

"One of them," Nan said, also grinning.

"Wait, who is that?" Leticia asked, leaning forward, and twisting her gaze to see better. “Oh. My. God! That is a great surprise."

Nan giggled and I think I did too.

We were all filled with joy at what was in front of us. A group of people we loved, who were our adopted family: Trunk and Suzie Halston and a few of their helpers; Compton, who looked more the farmer than the survivalist, with his arm around Patsy; and finally, Joey and Chloe. In Chloe's arms was their new baby, Joey Ronald Rancone.

We were home.

The End (of our beginning)

Thank you for reading
PERDITION: Ashfall Apocalypse 3

Please tell me if you would like the story to continue, and if so, which character you'd like to see more. Do this by providing a rating on Amazon and Goodreads and writing a review with this info.

Epilogue

Leticia - Three Months Later

It's crop rotation time, and that means a lot of work for everyone.

But no one complains. Everyone enjoys the work, even me.

Though my chores make it hard to find time to write, except during the evenings. And even then, I'm so tired, I'd rather sleep. Today was different because Ron let me stop early. So I have a lot of catching up to do.

This past week has been really cold. Yesterday, it was twenty-below. Mr. Halston said, before the ash fell, the coldest he'd ever experienced was fifteen degrees above zero. I shudder to think of what the temperatures are like now in Wyoming. They probably have the same geothermal vents as us, but they could never go outside.

Despite the low temperatures and with a lot of help from the Halstons, our new home was completed, and we moved in three days ago. So now Ronald, Nan, Sir Lancelot and I live in one house, a short walk from the Halston's home, where Chloe, Joey and Joey Jr. live.

The bigger news is that Ronald and Nan want to formally adopt me as their daughter. I cried when they told me this. They said since we had no government in which to file documents any longer, they would do some sort of ceremony before God, overseen by Mr. Halston as officiant. It would be "like a wedding," Nan said. I'm holding out for a true wedding ceremony for both of them.

They hold hands, like they're a couple. And I've seen them kiss. So, it could happen pretty soon. The big hold up was Ronald. Of that I'm sure.

Like all of us, his world changed when the volcanic ash began to fall. I would argue, it's when Ronald fell too. But also like the rest of us, he has come out of it a better man. We will never forget the people we lost. But it is our friends, especially those who have shared in our struggles, who make us better people.

Ronald and Nan have done that for me: made me better. They won't ever be replacements for my parents. More so it's like I will have two sets of parents: my first ones—who will always be in my heart— and now Ronald and Nan.

Likewise, Nan will not be a replacement for Liz, who will always be in Ronald's heart. But Nan would be his current wife, when he's ready. She definitely makes him better just as he has made her better too.

Reminds me of the cliché: What doesn't kill you will make you stronger. The ashfall apocalypse didn't kill us, but it definitely made each of us stronger.

And that leads me to my next piece of big news. I've decided to convert all my audio into a written book. It's our story of what happened after the apocalypse.

Of course, I'm calling it, Ashfall Apocalypse.

From the Author

Most of us prefer happy endings. But was this realistic?

I had written a different Epilogue which I ended up not using. Perhaps one day it will be part of another book.

Care to read it?

Simply go here:

https://www.subscribepage.com/ashfall3

Then give me your email address and I'll email it to you. And please tell me what you thought of it. Whatever you do, please don't reveal anything to others.

Again, thank you for reading!

MLB

Who is ML Banner?

Michael "ML" Banner is an award winning, USA Today Bestselling author of Apocalyptic Thrillers

Michael writes what he loves to read: apocalyptic thrillers, which thrust regular people into extraordinary circumstances, where their actions may determine not only their own fate, but that of the world. His work is traditionally published and self-published.

Often his thrillers are set in far-flung places, as Michael uses his experiences from visiting other countries—some multiple times—over the years. The picture was from a transatlantic cruise that became the foreground of his award-winning MADNESS Series.

When not writing his next book, you might find Michael (and his wife) traveling abroad or reading a Kindle, with his toes in the water (name of his publishing company), of a beach on the Sea of Cortez (Mexico).

Want more from M.L. Banner?

MLBanner.com

Receive FREE books & Apocalyptic Updates - A monthly publication highlighting discounted books, cool science/discoveries, new releases, reviews, and more

Connect with M.L. Banner

Keep in contact – I would love to hear from you!
Email: michael@mlbanner.com
Facebook: facebook.com/authormlbanner
Twitter: @ml_banner

Books by M.L. Banner

For a complete list of Michael's current and upcoming books: MLBanner.com/books/

ASHFALL APOCALYPSE

Ashfall Apocalypse (01)
A world-wide apocalypse has just begun.
Leticia's Soliloquy (An Ashfall Apocalypse Short)

Leticia tells her story.
(This short is exclusively available from link at end book #1)

Collapse (02)
As temps plummet, a new foe seeks revenge.
Compton's Epoch (An Ashfall Apocalypse Short)

Compton reveals what makes him tick.
(This short is exclusively available from link at end book #2)

Perdition (03)
Sometimes the best plan is to run. But where?

MADNESS CHRONICLES

MADNESS (01)
A parasitic infection causes mammals to attack.

PARASITIC (02)
The parasitic infection doesn't just affect animals.

SYMPTOMATIC (03)
When your loved one becomes symptomatic, what do you do?

The Final Outbreak (Books 1 - 3)
The end is coming. It's closer than you think. And it's real.

HIGHWAY SERIES

True Enemy (Short)
An unlikely hero finds his true enemy.
(Get this USA Today Bestselling short only on mlbanner.com)

Highway (01)
A terrorist attack forces siblings onto a highway, and an impossible journey home.

Endurance (02)
Enduring what comes next will take everything they've got, and more.
Resistance (03)
Coming Soon

STONE AGE SERIES

Stone Age (01)
The next big solar event separates family and friends, and begins a new Stone Age.

Desolation (02)
To survive the coming desolation will require new friendships.
Max's Epoch (Stone Age Short)
Max wasn't born a prepper, he was forged into one.
(This short is exclusively available on MLBanner.com)

Hell's Requiem (03)
One man struggles to survive and find his way to a scientific sanctuary.

Time Slip (Stand Alone)
The time slip was his accident; can he use it to save the one he loves?

Cicada (04)

The scientific community of Cicada may be the world's only hope,
or it may lead to the end of everything.

Made in the USA
Middletown, DE
19 May 2025

75738118R00146